30

D0238438

HARINGEY LIBRARIES

THIS BOOK MUST BE RETURNED ON OR BEFORE
THE LAST DATE MARKED BELOW

RAGING TEXAS

Connie Wheeler, the owner of the Thief Creek Hotel, was looking ahead to when her husband returned home. But Wheeler wasn't coming home, and it was left to Cord Mitchell — the man who'd killed him — to come and tell her how he'd died. His grim duty over, Mitchell was ready to ride on when, overnight, the hotel became the destination of Big Max and his gang of desperadoes, a condemned killer and his escort, plus a boatload of trouble. There was no way this Texan loner could quit until the trouble was over and Thief Creek ran red with blood . . .

MATT JAMES

RAGING TEXAS

Complete and Unabridged

LINFORD
Leicester

First published in Great Britain in 2003 by
Robert Hale Limited
London

First Linford Edition
published 2004
by arrangement with
Robert Hale Limited
London

British Library CIP Data

James, Matt
Raging Texas.—Large print ed.—
Linford western library
1. Western stories
2. Large type books
I. Title
823.9′2 [F]

ISBN 1–84395–517–2

Published by
F. A. Thorpe (Publishing)
Anstey, Leicestershire
Set by Words & Graphics Ltd.
Anstey, Leicestershire
Printed and bound in Great Britain by
T. J. International Ltd., Padstow, Cornwall

This book is printed on acid-free paper

1

Blood and Rain

*It was all in the touch with a deck or
  the dice,
And Mitchell the gambler had the
  sure touch . . .*

It took him some time to realize he was being followed.

On quitting the Silver Shell gambling hall on Corpus Christi's brightly lit Texas Avenue, Mitchell had shrugged comfortably into his worn gray mackinaw, tugged hatbrim low against the rain and set out for his railroad hotel without a thought for anything much beyond the fact that he had won big, had drunk some good bourbon and now felt like a walk in the rain to clear his head and savor his good fortune.

1

He took two side streets that led him away from the bright lights towards the grittier side of town. His hotel was the kind of place which a man temporarily low on funds might select upon his arrival in a strange town, the big hope being that if Lady Luck smiled, he might find himself checking out smartly to move into something fancier up on Main Street where the maids were prettier and the wallpaper not so faded.

It was hissing down now but, being a big winner, he found even the weather to his liking. Winners were grinners and losers could please themselves.

The moment he realized he'd picked up a tail the atmosphere of this invigorating Corpus Christi sea-rain seemed to alter. Suddenly it changed into a mizzle, a mean chilling bitch of a rain that whipped at the eyes and soaked his trouser cuffs as he halted beneath a dim and streaky streetlight to look back. Nothing stirred.

Nobody to be seen or heard but gloomy dark buildings, the distant clash of couplings at the switching yards and the drumming patter of the rain.

Another man might have shrugged, decided his instincts had played him false and moved on. Not Cord Mitchell.

Instead he turned away from the mouth of the high-walled, narrow alleyway ahead, and eased into a recessed doorway, dark and damp. There the gambling drifter remained totally motionless and silent, trusting in his instincts. Sometimes when he found himself on a cold and rainy night in a town he had never been in before, with whiskey on his breath and a fat roll riding his hip, instincts and Sam Colt were about all a man could rely on.

He sensed someone was back there in the Texas night and he wasn't about to budge until sure one way or the other.

To him, it figured naturally if someone was dogging him; it had to be in some way connected with the poker game at the Silver Shell he'd just quit.

The gambling hall was big, noisy and

glittery in a trashy kind of way. Patrons here were only interested in filling straights and being dealt pat hands, not style or decor. There'd been six players in all, a couple of very good ones and the others just average. Suckers. Large pots were the order of the night and Mitchell had only managed to chalk up the occasional winning hand during the first couple of hours, until suddenly it hit him.

The hot feeling.

All gamblers knew it, and even though he was not a full-time pro he could still identify it at first sign. It came as a sudden jolt that might strike you at any stage of any game, whether it be with cards, dice or wheel, a sudden certain sureness that you were on a roll and ready to streak.

Rarely did a seasoned player expect the lightning bolt to strike when down on his luck, a pessimism based on the old hustler's axiom that scared money never wins. But Cord Mitchell was a different kind of player. He was always ready for the roller-coaster of good fortune to start boosting him upwards, and so immediately began upping his bets and taking risks where he'd played close to the vest before. And couldn't lose for winning.

He finally quit with several hundred riding his hip pocket, the old pros wryly envious and the big losers morose and silent as he promised to return the following night to give them a chance to get it back.

And now, with a rivulet of cold rain water trickling down his mackinaw collar and the alley-mouth beckoning, he pictured the three big losers in his mind's eye: the fat farmer from inland, the tall and flashy hotelkeeper from someplace down south, the traveller in ladies' bonnets living it up on his monthly visit from Fort Worth.

Which of that trio might be dumb or reckless enough to take his gambling losses so badly as to take off after the big winner with something foolish in mind?

He shook his head.

None, if he was any judge. Yet it had to be the money. Unless of course he'd simply attracted the attention of some Corpus Christi petty thief down on his luck. His jaws set tightly. He hadn't journeyed a hundred miles and labored long and patiently at the unforgiving tables to finally conjure up a lucky streak and ride it home in style, simply to provide meth money for some rod-riding hobo with more ambition than good sense. If there was someone back there, heavyweight heller or ragged-assed sneak thief, he would take him on on his terms and choose the battleground.

Defiantly, he swung away into the alley and began striding it out, a tall figure in a flapping mackinaw now with one hand resting on gunbutt. He wouldn't hurry. He seldom went looking for trouble but by the same token would not be harried, hurried or pushed around. This was his night with his honest earnings snug against his backside. If that shadow back there followed him in here there could be trouble. Trouble for the shadow.

He glanced over his shoulder, propped. There it was. The silhouetted figure was outlined against the misted glare of that solitary streetlamp. By this time Mitchell was half-way down the long alley where the light was dimmest. The rain had eased and it had gone quiet over at the yards. Now he could hear the man's steps. They were slightly uneven, as if he had been running or was drunk.

Then he saw the gun.

The watery light glinted dully along the barrel for just a split second. But that was enough. In one oiled motion, Cord Mitchell came clear and stepped back two paces to get his back against a dripping wall.

'Freeze right there!' he warned, the rearing buildings funnelling the sound of his voice.

The figure stopped and slipped into a crouch.

'Throw the money on the ground and hightail!' he was ordered in a vaguely familiar voice. The gun waved impatiently. 'I mean business, Mitchell, I'm a desperate man!'

Cord's scalp pulled tight as he eased his gun hammer back. 'Miller?' he called. Miller was the fat man from inland who'd dropped close to a hundred.

'Do as I say, damn you. Drop the dough.'

Recognition hit with a jolt. 'Wheeler!' It wasn't Miller but the hard-jawed hotel man from the south. The heaviest loser of the night and certainly the sorest. Mitchell amended that latter thought as he slowly raised his cutter. Not just maybe — definitely the sorest as he now recalled. 'Don't be a fool, man. You lost fair and square and — '

'And you talk too much, Mitchell. Do as I say or by God I'll let you have it.'

'You'll never see home again if you — '

The shimmering sunburst of the deafeningly exploding Colt .45 illuminated the space between fast-ducking Mitchell and sore loser Wheeler. Above the roar, Cord heard his own sharp intake of breath as something lethal whipped past his neck and whammed into the wall behind, zinging off wildly. He was ready to let fly in retaliation when the shout sounded from the street.

'Drop those guns. This is the law!'

But a second bullet was already snarling its venomous way towards Mitchell. He dived low and forward, hit the ground rolling and fanned gun hammer, holding the trigger back tightly and banging the hammer back with the left palm twice in such rapid succession that it sounded as one ugly bellow of sound.

Two bullets and two square hits.

The sheer impact of the lead lifted Wheeler off his feet, hurling him up against the side wall of a supply shed, his face an awful, sudden white. He triggered just once more, the slug ploughing into the ground between his widespread boots with a jarring thud.

Mitchell did not shoot again. He knew where his lead had gone.

Wheeler began struggling as though with an invisible adversary, choking and gurgling. He staggered forward through wreathing gunsmoke, his eyes fixed on slow-rising Mitchell. He pitched forward and he hit hard with blood trickling from his mouth. He was still breathing as Mitchell reached him to turn him on his side. His hands clawed at Cord's shirt front, his eyes wide with horror.

'My wife and boy, Mitchell . . . tell them it was all for them. All . . . '

He was still clutching Mitchell's shirt front when a final jolting surge of energy ran through him, enabling him almost to rise on one knee.

Then his whole body snapped taut, went limp, and he was dead.

★   ★   ★

10

If you had to kill a man and wanted an eyewitness, about the best kind you could have had to be a city marshal.

'I was tipped off there might be trouble following the big game at the Silver Shell,' muttered the tall, mustached peace officer, studying Mitchell's papers. 'Er . . . Mr Mitchell.' He looked up, hazel eyes mirroring the overhead lamps of the law office. 'I'm sorry I caught up with you and Wheeler too late to avoid . . . '

His words tapered off. There was a body in the morgue. A low wind moaned fitfully about the windows. And Cord Mitchell was visibly still affected by that lurid moment of violence back in the alley. It went without saying that everybody was sorry, the peace officer thought bitterly. In particular Mr Thaddeus Wheeler of the Thief Creek Hotel and Trailhouse, Storm Bay.

These were the details the peace officer read out from bloodstained documents found upon the body. There was also a photograph in the billfold which he passed wordlessly across the desk for Mitchell's perusal.

Cord winced as though in pain.

The picture showed the dead man, tall and smiling, standing before a two-storied building with one arm about the shoulders of a dark-haired and serious-looking woman, his other hand resting on the shoulder of the child standing before them.

'Anything else to make me feel worse?' Mitchell's tone was bitter. 'Pillar of the church, maybe? Gave half his earnings to the poor? Most popular man in Texas?'

'No . . . just an everyday family man at this stage.' The lawman paused to check out another slip of paper. 'And according to this letter from his wife postmarked the eighth, was up to his ears in debt and was in this city looking to raise bank capital to bail them out. Want some coffee?'

Mitchell shook his head. No.

What he really wanted was about twelve

hours' sleep following his twenty-mile ride to Corpus Christi followed by a fifteen-hour session at the poker tables. And, oh yes, a killing to round it all off.

'Guess you're new to this sort of thing,' the lawman remarked, rising to move across to the pot belly. From the appearance of the jailhouse coffee he poured they should serve it by the slice.

Mitchell did not answer. As a thirty-five-year-old man without a star, he'd seen his share of troubles and then some. But it was a long time since some fool had forced him into a corner where the only choice was kill or be killed. His plan right now was to finalize the necessary formalities, then go get a bottle, drink it, sleep it off, then quit Corpus Christi at daybreak, hopefully with a blank mind and clear conscience.

He only wished the marshal had not left that opened billfold facing up on his desk that way.

He leaned forward to take another reluctant look, and grimaced.

That kid looked about six or seven years of age.

'Every working man thinks his job is the toughest, Mr Mitchell,' the marshal philosophized, returning to his chair. 'I'm no different to the rest. This is a tough job. But you know the hardest part of it all? No, not facing down liquored-up hellions trying to murder you, horning in on domestic disputes, or even fishing corpses out of the water. The worst by far is knocking on some door in the middle of the night to tell someone a loved one won't be coming back — ever.'

The lawman sighed and downed some of his cold and ultra-thick black coffee.

'Lucky for me this lady . . . ' he put on his eyeglasses to scan those bloodied documents once more. 'Ah, yes — Mrs Connie Wheeler of Storm Bay — lives beyond my area of jurisdiction, meaning I can fob off reporting her husband's death to her personally on to the sheriff down at Bell's Landing.' He removed his spectacles and looked Mitchell straight in the eye. 'That's what I call luck, don't you, Mr Mitchell?'

'Maybe I'd better handle that job, Marshal,' Mitchell was astonished to hear himself blurt out. 'Seeing as I did the killing, that is . . . '

Standing outside the imposing white-painted law office some time later, with the Gulf wind blowing papers across the empty street, Cord Mitchell wondered what had made him do it. Not shoot that man down; that had been inevitable. But what in the name of all that was holy had compelled him to offer to discharge the marshal's duty for him by volunteering to inform that woman of her husband's ugly death?

Cord Wheeler was a life-hardened loner and by no stretch of the imagination any kind of humanitarian who normally went about doing good deeds. He was much more inclined by nature to drink up any stray dollar he might have in his pocket rather than hand it to a starving hobo on the street. Tough enough by any yardstick, he was selfish and self-reliant and had always had to be that way, always on the look-out for *numero uno*. So how come he had been suddenly moved to cast himself in the totally unfamiliar role of the Good Samaritan — had actually volunteered for it?

What was he seeking? Forgiveness? Understanding? He would be lucky if he didn't get shot for his troubles, he brooded, for he was yet to meet one wife or sweetheart of any two-bit gambler or sore loser who failed to perceive her man as a cross between John the Baptist and El Cid — after some civic-minded citizen had blown him, Jack, Clint or Amos, out of his boots.

So, if he didn't expect anything good, could it be that he was deliberately sticking his neck out in the hope of attracting something bad at Storm Bay? Perhaps he was seeking condemnation and even some kind of punishment which might somehow purge him of the guilt he'd accrued in killing that man and leaving his family to fend for itself in a harsh world.

Could it be that Cord Mitchell, world weary man of the West, aimlessly working his way down the Texas coastline towards the tip-end of America, might be actually searching for absolution for this and other sins in order that he might get to sleep more peacefully than he had done these many lone-riding years?

Cord Mitchell shouldn't think so much, he lectured himself gravely and headed off slowly down the brooding street to buy that bottle for the journey. Or maybe two.

2

Storm Brewin'

'Big wind comin'!' Joachim bawled across the yard. 'Go get your coat, boy.'

'Get the goat, Joe?' Jody shouted back cheekily. 'The goat's in the pen already.'

'Smart shrimps get their tails paddled.'

'The pails are tallied,' the boy replied, deliberately misinterpreting, one hand cocked to his ear as though having trouble hearing. 'See?' He indicated the stack of pails standing in their rack by the wagon-shed doors.

With a snort of disgust the Thief Creek Hotel's cook, handyman, roustabout and weather expert swung his broad back and started off up the steps. The mid-morning stage from Kingsville was due in shortly, and passengers and crew would be ravening for breakfast. But before vanishing inside, the sturdy French-Texan with the broad brown face and the Indian-style plaited hair, paused to gaze out over the familiar sweeps of the bay, sniffing the turbulent air and reading the signs as only a long-time coast-dweller could.

Joachim could smell the change in the weather, had been watching for it all morning ever since quitting his house-boat for the short row across Thief Creek to the hotel landing. The pressure in the air affected his ears, and the sunlight looked milky and shot with haze.

Bad weather always came abruptly to that country this time of year. It could be balmy autumn one morning, then by noon the sky would darken and purple, and evening would bring the wintry rain.

Joachim had told his woman that morning that it would soon rain and keep raining. That the wind would rise and swing around from the south, cut across to the west and come finally from the north. It would there gather its forces, growling and gusting and causing storm warnings to go up right down the coast from Louisiana to Brownsville before hurtling its full fury southwards, gathering force and fury as it roared towards Padre Island, the Laguna Madre and Storm Bay. Water in Owl Marsh would form surf-lines in foamy ridges and break over the grass, sluicing back and forth, whipping up debris and foam. There would be blackbirds, tossing like chips in the cold wind and ducks flying low as folks put up their storm shutters and battened down — that's if they had sense enough not to ignore the signals. Joachim snorted.

Some people wouldn't sense weather coming in even if they found themselves up to their necks in floodwaters.

He whirled sharply and unexpectedly to catch a glimpse of the boy hanging upside down by his heels on the pen fence, tormenting the goat.

'Dumb kid!'

The booming voice caused Jody to lose concentration. He slipped down on to his head and the goat tried to butt him as he jumped to his feet.

Joachim's broad face wore a self-satisfied smile as he vanished inside to make ready for the invasion by the carrion-eaters aboard the southbound stage.

The kid was butted twice before managing to clamber from the goat pen. Animal and child shared a hate-hate relationship, the boy being exuberant and full of mischief while the goat was aged, venerable and characteristically goat-like, short tempered.

Jody picked a handful of nettles and thrust them through the slats of the pen. The goat, short-sighted and foolish, took a mouthful then backed up, snorting with irritation as the boy ran off giggling, feeling honor had been vindicated.

He was scooting round the stables' corner when he almost cannoned into the woman with the egg basket coming the other way.

'Jody! Why don't you look where you're going?'

'Sorry, Mom. What's for breakfast?'

'You've already had it,' the woman said, heading across the blowing yard for the hotel with her son tagging along. 'Oatmeal.'

'Oatmeal ain't breakfast.'

'And don't say ain't. How many times must I tell you.'

The boy stopped and watched his mother's tall angular figure beat its way across to the big, badly painted hotel and vanish inside. He kicked a stone and pouted. His mom wasn't fun anymore. Never had time to play or to gather him up and give him huge hugs these days. Not like before — before they had come here to the bay.

Jody calculated it must be around two years now since they had shifted to the coast from West Texas. At first his parents seemed happy, taking over the hotel and trailhouse, meeting new people and talking about fish and house-guests and suchlike 'most all the time.

But it had not been very happy for a long time now, and in his child mind he sensed that his mother's testiness now had to do with his father being away for longer than she'd expected. He had heard her discussing his father with Joachim yesterday, and she sounded angry and almost as if she was about to cry.

A sea bird's sudden shriek interrupted his thoughts and he looked round to see the coach from Kingsville swinging in off the Gilmour Trail, Old Ethan the driver bringing the equipage in swiftly and neatly right at the hotel steps.

Jody ran across to watch the passengers disembark for breakfast while the hostler changed the sweating horses.

There was a gaunt man in black frock-coat and top hat, two very fat ladies with red faces who talked a lot, a sad-eyed man with a bottle protruding from his pocket and an old woman who had to be toted inside by the driver and guard. No kids to play with. Again.

Seemed to him children hardly ever travelled along the trail these days. Maybe they were scared of Indians or something. He was not afraid of anything or anybody, except perhaps Mom when she got mad. He was going to be an Indian fighter when he grew up and shoot as many red devils as he could. He liked saying 'red devils' even though his mother always got sore at him for it.

He sat playing with the dog and watching the rolling clouds as the stage finally pulled out with the old lady complaining loudly and bitterly about the coffee being too cold, the pie too hot, and didn't anyone on God's earth care about her lumbago?

The coach rocked away, climbing for the trail with the buckskinned driver hunched over the reins and the big gun-guard with the black mustache clutching his sawed off in the upright position in mute warning to road agents everywhere.

As the sound of hoofs and wheels faded to the south, the boy turned his curly head to see his mother standing at the top of the steps, gazing off into the squally north beyond the distant town.

Jody could tell by her look just what she was thinking about. Not the coach just gone or the next one which wouldn't show until morning. Nor even hot scones or cold coffee. This was her fretting look. His father had been gone too long. There had been fights before he left; there were always fights these days. Jody was used to them, was getting to think this was how all married folks lived. Seemed to him that whatever his father did his mother found fault with these days. He'd asked Joachim about it but he had just shrugged and made some deep observation on human beings and married folks which went clean over the boy's head.

Eventually Connie Wheeler sighed

and disappeared inside to help Joachim and their staff of just two clean up after the invasion.

The dog came up to the boy and began slobbering all over him. Cody made a sixgun shape with forefinger and thumb and went 'Pow! Got you right between the eyes, you red devil.'

He was trying to educate the dog to play dead when he shot him but it just began licking him instead. They were wrestling when he saw the jackass in the corral across the yard prick its ears sharply. Jody pushed the dog away and got to his feet as the horseman showed beyond the shoulder of the hill where the stage trail looped in.

The boy frowned. A guest, he thought. Mom would be happy about that. This time of year the guests just about stopped coming altogether, leaving only the stages and the occasional trail traveller to rely upon. By midwinter the hotel's fourteen rooms, ten up and four down, would all be empty and Jody would have free run of the echoing place, which was how he liked it.

As the rider came in through the gate he saw he was tall and lean in quiet gray clothes and broad-brimmed hat. It was hard to tell if he was old or young; he looked like someone who rarely smiled. His hair was black, his eyes were blue and Jody was happy to see he sported a sixgun thonged to his thigh, suggesting he might prove to be a real buckaroo. 'Hi, mister,' he called. But the rider trotted straight by him, eyes on the upper floor of the hotel. If little Jody Wheeler was any judge of human nature, this tall stranger had something on his mind.

He hoped it was trouble. There was never enough trouble at the Thief Creek Hotel and Trailhouse to suit the boy, even if others might think there was, and always had been, far too much.

★　★　★

Discordant sounds reached Mitchell, seated uncomfortably on an unpadded chair in the office as he waited: sparrows in the oaks, the distant horn of a ship passing the mouth of the bay, metallic hammering from the barn across the yard. He was waiting for the woman to weep but it was growing plainer by the moment this wasn't about to happen. Connie Wheeler sat very erect at her desk examining the items he'd brought with him: documents, rings, letters, a billfold. An empty billfold. Her face looked similarly empty, pale and expressionless.

The new widow was a tall slender woman with long brown arms and legs. Her face was olive brown with high cheeks, dark eyes beneath black, slightly arched brows. Her lips were full and her teeth small and white. She wore a faded gingham dress with a ribbon belt. The dress had once been green with a pattern of pink roses on it.

'Thank you, Mr Mitchell,' she said finally.

'You're welcome.'

'I take it you knew my husband in

Corpus Christi?'

'Some. I was, er . . . at the gambling hall the night he was, er . . . '

'Shot.'

'Yes.'

'Do the authorities know who killed my husband?'

'He was well liked up there, ma'am. Respected.'

'There's no need for you to try to find things to say that might soften the blow, Mr Mitchell,' Connie Wheeler said, rising a little stiffly from behind her desk. 'My husband was neither well liked nor widely respected. He had ways that irritated people. He was constantly building himself up and boasting about his achievements when everyone knew he was just a simple hotel proprietor and not a very successful one at that.'

Mitchell made no reply.

The woman stood at the window gazing out across the nearby headland of Devil's Spur towards Owl Marsh. The back wall of the building needed paint. From the hotel grounds an expanse of flat, reddish clay reached several hundred yards to a sagging wire fence. Beyond the fence lay the marsh, dry and cracked like dirty china in the summer months but dark and flooding as winter drew on.

Mitchell obliquely studied her back, lean and straight, as she continued to stare out.

From where he sat he could see the birds above the high stone comb of the spur. The rain was bringing them in off the Gulf. There were gulls and redwing blackbirds, solitary cranes and sand-pipers, all following the water as it moved in and out with the tide.

He knew birds but obviously not as much about women as he might have thought.

Suddenly she turned sharply.

'I must say I'm surprised that a total stranger should take on the duty of delivering tidings of this nature, Mr Mitchell.' She puckered her brow at him. 'Don't you find it a little odd yourself? By your own admission, you were only a gambling associate of my husband, and I'm sure we all know that such associations mean nothing. You don't know us, and it's normally the duty of the authorities to handle notifications. I'm sure you understand my confusion?'

Cord Mitchell had an excellent poker face. He could be sitting on a straight flush with a $500 pot in the center yet still look as though all he was wondering about was if his horse might be in need of a saddle blanket that night. That look was firmly and impassively in place as he drew the makings from a jacket pocket and commenced rolling a durham.

'I was heading this way, I felt bad about him dying the way he did, they told me he had a family . . . ' He shrugged. 'So I offered. Of course if this upsets you, ma'am — '

'No, no of course not. I really am very grateful.' She paused, arms folded. 'That surely sounds odd, doesn't it?

Expressing gratitude for news that should make any normal person feel exactly the opposite?'

Mitchell said nothing. Although rarely troubled by guilt it was something uncomfortably akin to that emotion which had brought him here to Storm Bay, and it was gnawing away at him now as he licked tobacco and paper into a neat white cylinder and sat studying the result.

He knew Wheeler had given him no option but to cut him down. The man had been ready to murder him for a few lousy dollars. Neither the city marshal nor anyone else had pointed a finger of blame in his direction over the gun-down. So why had he not let it lie there? Now he was here in the building where Wheeler had lived his life, had seen his wife and child — but had yet to admit to the part he had played in the man's death.

And wasn't that the real reason he'd made his offer to the Corpus Christi marshal? Had he not originally intended to seek out the widow to explain exactly what had happened in that rain-swept alleyway in order that she would understand and maybe not feel so bad?

A discreet tap sounded on the office door and the hotel maid entered with a tray bearing coffee-pot and cups. Her timing was bad. Mitchell had been ready to get up, excuse himself and go throw a leg over his horse and travel. Why didn't he leave now anyway?

Maybe he was waiting for Connie Wheeler to finally break down and cry. Then again it could have been he was looking for something that might somehow make him feel better about taking a woman's husband and a kid's father, before pushing on south to wherever it was he might be heading.

It was a half-hour later before Cord Mitchell quit the office to accompany the woman out to the desk, where she signed him in for an overnight stay in room 22 upstairs.

He didn't bother trying to figure why he'd made the strange decision to stay over. He simply knew, in light of what he'd seen, of a business plainly just hanging on by its fingernails and stuck out here on its lonesome miles from the nearest town on a bluff overlooking a place appropriately named Storm Bay, that he didn't want to just ride off right away. It was as simple or as complicated as that.

Later as he stood smoking by his window watching big dark clouds rolling down the coast of Texas in the afternoon, he heard the sounds of a child's sobbing from someplace below.

Mitchell fingertipped a fragment of tobacco from his lip. At least someone seemed sad Thad Wheeler was gone.

★ ★ ★

Joachim rarely slept. Most nights after a long day at the hotel, instead of rowing around the brooding spur to his houseboat and the Indian woman he lived with, he would instead go poling down to the marsh to hunt for crabs and shrimp.

The weather never bothered him and he was as much at home with the frothy waves roiling and crashing against the beach as he was on calm blue summer nights, slapping mosquitoes, baiting his hooks and keeping company with his best friends, his private thoughts.

It was a little after midnight when he returned to the hotel jetty with the tide and the wind behind him. He knelt in the boat, poling, with his rifle laid across the boat and the hotel dog seated in the bow.

He gathered up a dripping sack of oysters and tied up before stepping out. He looked south. The water was spilling across the marsh as the tide moved in, spreading swiftly through the grass hummocks, receding slowly.

When he turned his head towards the bulk of the hotel he saw lights were still burning, as he expected.

It was a black day for them all even if not totally unexpected for big brown Joachim. Although long since tamed by the years, he had lived wild and free once, understood men and what made them do things. Deep down, he realized he'd always half-expected Miss Connie's husband to land in deep water one day. He'd been too hungry, too jittery and in many ways too foolish not to. But he'd never expected it could end so suddenly and brutally, leaving him feeling a sense of even greater responsibility toward those left behind.

With a sigh he set out for the hotel buildings along the jetty plankwalk with the dog running ahead of him. He took his catch to the meathouse, then went to the stables to check on his mule. The buckskin stared at him over the half-door of its stall, its rolling eye like a blob of tallow in the glow of the night-light.

Joachim studied the guest's horse thoughtfully. Funny about Mitchell, he mused. He didn't look like a man much given to good works and kind deeds. What he looked like to Joachim was a tolerably tough man maybe wearied down some by life. Quietly spoken yet reassuring in his manner, Mitchell seemed like someone who'd seen it all, whom life and events had shaped a certain way, as Joachim was aware they had also shaped himself.

Yet for some reason he was pleased the man had decided to check in. With just himself and the young working couple, Jinko and Mary, to keep Miz Connie and the kid company on this darkest of all nights, it helped to have someone else around, especially a man obviously concerned about the disaster that had overtaken the Thief Creek Hotel family.

Connie was the only one still up when he entered the lobby, smelling of fishy things and of the marsh. She was seated at the desk going through her husband's papers, glancing up vaguely as Joachim crossed to her in his big heavy boots.

'Tide's up,' he grunted.

'Hmm . . . '

'Tide's up, it's gone midnight and it's time you were abed, Miz Connie.'

She put down a pen and fingered her eyes. 'I suppose you're right, Joe.' Then she frowned at him. 'Gone midnight and you still haven't even been home? Are you quite sure you're not part swamp 'gator or something?'

'No call for you to put on a brave face for me, Miz Connie.'

She rose sharply.

'I am not putting on a brave anything.' She indicated the papers. 'I'm simply doing what must be done in light of what's happened.' She paused, then went on. 'Mr Mitchell says the body will arrive from Corpus Christi within the next couple of days . . . '

'Mighty bad thing, Miz Connie, mighty bad.'

Connie came out from behind the desk. The wind was buffeting the frame building and rattling the shutters. She looked along the hallway leading to the ground-floor rooms and her private quarters.

'I very much doubt Thad secured the loan money he was looking for,' she said slowly, running her hands through her hair. 'Which means — '

'Which means we'll get along here the same as we always have,' Joachim said firmly. 'I'll take care of the lights, Miz Connie.'

She smiled gratefully, wearily, as she turned away. Moving down the hallway, Connie Wheeler was suddenly aware of the slow thudding of her own heart. The day had been an eternity long and she could never remember having felt so tired as she entered her son's room to check on him.

Jody was asleep with tear-stains on his cheeks. She kissed him and went through to her room and threw herself across the bed.

It began as a sharp pain in the pit of her stomach, then rose in her throat, hot and stinging. Then it broke, as something shatters its shell and bursts outwards. She buried her face in her arms and just cried, yet none of her tears were for her dead husband. She'd stopped weeping over him years before.

3

Waitin' For The Man

He did not attend the funeral. Instead, several days into his stayover at the hotel, Cord Mitchell donned moleskins and sheepskin jacket and went walking on the southern side of Storm Bay on the morning that, on the north, the mortal remains of Thaddeus Wheeler were being lowered into the good earth at the Bell's Landing cemetery.

He felt curiously detached from what was going on over there as he made his way along the shoreline by Devil's Spur. It was a big blustery day with occasional rain squalls and for him it seemed enough just to accept the day on its own terms and relax in a way he really hadn't done since hammering two bullets into Wheeler's chest.

A flight of ducks rose suddenly before him. They got up in a leaping, noisy burst of alarm, beating away until falling into a flight pattern which carried them out over the water, skimming the surface.

The dog was with him. He appeared to have made a big hit with the dog and the kid, but otherwise found himself treated with a wary reserve like someone important whose business they might not quite approve of.

Whether Connie, Joachim or the hotel couple suspected anything unusual or even ulterior in his continuing presence, he had no idea.

Of course if they were simply puzzled why a man alone would choose to stop over at the hotel long after the holiday season was past, this only meant they were in the same category as himself.

He didn't know either. Yet he was determined not to ruin this opportunity to enjoy a fine easy day by trying to figure that puzzle out for himself right now. He was here, the blustery weather suited his frame of mind, eventually he would go. That was how things were and he was content to accept them that way for now.

The tan-and-white hound scooted on ahead as he passed along the beachfront and the long, rickety jetty beneath the gaunt and brooding landmark of the spur. Devil's Spur was well named. The headland appeared as if it had been deliberately fashioned by nature to appear huge, evil and threatening, then had been subjected to a few thousand years of rough weather and winter winds to lend it an air of mystery and character.

Errant sounds reached him as he sighted the houseboat tied up in the lee of the spur a hundred yards ahead. Seemed like the homey rattle of pots and pans. The dog wagged its tail and looked up at him. Cord shrugged, drove his hands deep into his pockets and headed for the jetty where the vessel was moored.

He hunched his shoulders as the

wind hit from a different angle. In knockabout rig he appeared larger and more rugged than in the plain gray suits. He was a tall man, solid of shoulder and flat of belly. He walked in an easy slouch right now, hips thrust forward, head tilted back. His regular, strong features, perhaps lined and creased a little more than they should be at thirty-five, were topped by thick black hair as coarse as a mare's mane which stubbornly resisted every attempt to tame it with brush, comb, scissors or pomade.

This was a man who mostly made his living indoors in gambling halls, business offices and trading stations, yet did his real living out under an open sky.

He was seeing everything with an outdoorsman's eyes; that the wind had fallen away some after driving down from the north for a week and more; where it had pushed the water out of the marsh towards the Gulf, laying bare an endless expanse of mud and wiry, stiff-grass hummocks.

There would be mullet in the shallows too, he surmised, driven by low water towards the coastal shelf.

Cord took a cigarette from his pocket and lighted it behind cupped hands, then set his boots on the jetty.

The Indian woman emerged from the house-boat and grunted, 'Breakfast ready, Mr Mitchell.'

Cord propped. Was he missing something here? Then she smiled.

'Joachim has told me all about you. When I see you come round the spur I know you come to visit Crow Woman.' Smile-wrinkles around dark eyes cut deeper. 'Nobody at hotel tell you much, so you come to me. So?'

How did she know all this?

Over a solid breakfast of fish fries and cornbread, he found out. Crow Woman had somehow gleaned from Joachim that while they found Mitchell a pleasant and welcome guest at the hotel, there seemed to be a question mark hanging over his ongoing presence, as there had been over the reason he had elected to be the one to bring the news of Wheeler's death to the Thief Creek.

So they treated him with polite respect, yet Crow Woman's instincts must have told her he needed something more.

'I will tell anyone anything just to keep them talking and so not leave me alone,' she said with that infectious smile. 'What does Mr Mitchell wish to know?'

He wanted to know about the Wheelers. And he found out. An unhappy marriage marred by the husband's unreliability, big ideas, bad habits and unreadiness to simply stay put and pitch in. This was Crow Woman's summary.

And the wife?

'The best of women,' he was told. 'But with too many burdens for one so young. I fear now she will lose the hotel. This will be very sad as she has worked so hard, but all is money, no? More cornbread?'

Cord Mitchell seemed to have lost his appetite. He'd set out in a positive frame of mind, with the vague intention of figuring out just why he was staying on, and to make a decision when he would quit.

Instead, by the time he got back to the hotel in late afternoon after hiking almost out to the ocean and back through the dunes, he was feeling bad again, a state of mind which was in no way improved when he arrived in time to see Connie and her staff catering for a coachload of stage passengers from the cattle country, while still attired in their mourning black.

A somber Joachim invited him to take a glass of something. He didn't need to be asked twice. Something warned him he should not drink today, but for perhaps the first time in a month, Cord Mitchell, though showing few outward signs, proceeded to really tie one on.

At dark he found himself in the big echoing dining-room playing Chinese checkers with Jody, a precocious little kid who seemed wise beyond his years and called him by his given name — just another reason, so it seemed, for whiskey-sipping Mitchell to feel a little worse than before.

When Connie entered the room to check on the child and ask 'Mr Mitchell' what he would like for supper, he cordially invited her also to address him as Cord. This she did, which for some perverse reason only goaded him into reaching for the bottle and pouring himself three fingers.

It was as though everyone was suddenly in a conspiracy to start treating guest Cord Mitchell as the family friend, with not a whisper of suspicion that he had blasted husband and father into eternity with his Colt .45 in a Corpus Christi alleyway following a poker game.

He'd been here three days and hadn't said one word about what had really happened.

He studied the child through narrowed eyes.

They had the right to know how Wheeler had died, he believed. So why had he, a usually direct and unemotional man, held back?

And a voice in the back of his mind whispered: 'Could it be you've taken a shine to the woman, Mitchell? That you don't want to give her cause to hate your guts?'

'No!' he said aloud, and Jody stared.

'Did I make the wrong move, Cord?'

Mitchell shook his head and rose from the table. 'No, of course not. I just said that because . . . because I can't believe a squirt kid can beat me so easily.'

'But the game's not over yet.'

It was for him.

He tousled the boy's curls and walked unsteadily from the room. At the doorway he paused to look back at Jody, deep lines cutting his cheeks as his thoughts went deep. He was thirty-five years of age. Half done. No wife, child or future. He'd thought Wheeler a failure and a fool, yet the man had done a lot more with his life than had he. Or at least that was how it suddenly appeared to the eyes of the man who'd killed him.

Impulsively he went searching for the woman even though every instinct warned him that what he should be doing was climbing those stairs to room 22 and sleeping it off.

When he sighted Connie out in the yard broad-casting grain for the chickens by the final dregs of daylight, Mitchell swung drunkenly but purposefully from the window only to find the stalwart figure of Joachim, still in dark garb, filling the doorway.

The two men traded stares and it seemed to Mitchell in his slightly befuddled condition that the other was watching him too closely, too searchingly.

'Mind stepping aside, Joe?'

'Guess I do mind, Mr Mitchell.'

Cord frowned uncertainly. 'Huh?' He cleared his throat. 'There's something I need to do — '

'You need go sleep it off.'

'Now look here, Joe, I need to see Mrs Wheeler and — '

'Make her day even worse than it has been?' Joachim shook his big brown head. 'No, can't agree that would be a good idea.'

Cord was getting riled.

'What are you talking about, man?'

'Why, about you telling Miz Connie something she doesn't really need to know, sir.'

Through a haze of alcohol fumes, Cord Mitchell could feel himself sobering a little as he understood what was being said. He was confused, puzzled and angry all at once.

'What are you saying?' he demanded, drawing himself up to his full height and putting on the glower he reserved for intimidating drunks in bar-rooms.

'You are going to tell her about killing Mr Wheeler, aren't you, Mr Mitchell?'

He was stunned.

'What . . . ? I mean, how in hell do you know?'

'My woman. She told me.'

'Crow Woman? That's a damn lie. I told her nothing.'

'Told her everything, I fear. You see, she's Comanche, sir. Full blood. Her father was the tribe's medicine man and she picked up a lot of his tricks. She can read a man's face like a book. If you rub your nose a certain way she knows you're telling a lie. Her speciality is killing something like a rat or a gopher, leaving it out all night with its belly sliced open, then she reads the entrails next morning and can tell you if it will rain next week or that your brother-in-law in Houston has just busted his leg.'

'Are you saying . . . ?'

'All them questions you asked her about the family and the marriage and the rest. Crow Woman said she knew almost before you'd finished your first mug of coffee that you'd killed Mr Wheeler and didn't know how to go about breaking the news here. Are you going to tell me she's wrong?'

Cord found himself shaking his head

slowly from side to side. No, he was not about to do that. Yet he felt curiously relieved that his secret was out at last.

'In that case,' he said quietly, 'it's best she hears it from me right now before she learns it from someone else.'

'She won't hear it from me or my woman.'

'She's going to hear it from me, then. Right now.'

He made to push by but a big hand stopped him.

'It was nice you coming here the way you did, Mr Mitchell. A stranger breaking sad news as kindly as you did. Miz Connie appreciated that. She likes you because she finds you a gentleman, was happy when you decided to stay on some. I don't want you to bust that bubble for her today.'

'Sorry, I've made up my mind. Step aside, Joe.'

'Can't do that, sir.'

Cord grabbed at the man's shoulder clumsily. The sound of Joachim's big bronzed fist clipping his jaw attracted the woman's attention as she came through the front doors from the yard. But by the time Connie Wheeler rounded the passageway corner by the staircase, Joachim was toting an unconscious Mitchell up the stairs.

'Joe!' she cried. 'What on earth . . . ?'

'Mr Mitchell's just had a little too much to drink, Miz Connie. He'll be fine when he sleeps it off.'

He was anything but fine when he awoke hours later, and it wasn't just the hangover. Now that he was sober and the Dutch courage the liquor had given him had vaporized, he knew he could not tell her. For some reason he could not get it out of his mind that Joachim had said she liked him.

He still had no idea why this should seem so important to him. For loner Cord Mitchell had never been in love before. Hadn't even been close.

★ ★ ★

A heavy-wheeled green Concord coach hitched to a double span of restless horses stood at the curb on Ocean Street, Diamondback, directly opposite the Chicken House and just around the corner from Downhill Avenue.

Ocean Street was not a good place to park late at night, or at any other time for that matter. But Downhill Avenue — and rarely was a South Texas street better named — was one hell of a lot worse.

From the intersection of Ocean and Downhill, this sprawling, overcrowded sea town went from crime, corruption and vice all the way down the social scale to abject poverty, mindless violence and total despair.

Respectable people had no business in Diamondback, which only added to its attraction for men with shady deals to hatch, grudges to even, scores to settle, crooked fortunes to make or talent to recruit.

The four men waiting in the darkened coach had all been recruited here, two from the 'classy' upper side and the others from lower Downhill Street, where, even in that cesspool of humanity where desperate people convulsed in a teeming life of crime and desperation, they had made their names, bossed their own fetid patch, stood taller than those about them simply because they were harder, stronger and always readier to kill.

Manny Clyde sat facing forward, manicuring his fingers with a tiny, gold-bladed penknife. An average-looking man, he wore expensive clothes which did not succeed in making him look anything but average. His only distinguishing features were the flat dark brows joined together like a band of iron across his brow. Although the party had been waiting here some time Clyde didn't look bored. Didn't look impatient either. He looked as though waiting for someone was a job he was trained for.

Frick sat at his side staring moodily at the gloomy street where drunks

55

weaved in and out of reeking dives and the honky tonk music never ceased. He looked big as a buffalo in a light grey raincoat belted tightly to show off the differential between enormous shoulders and trim waistline. Frick appeared rugged and fit, yet the only exercise he ever took was running from the law or beating up on people for fun or profit.

Seated knees-to-knees with Frick, Jim Joe Jackson from the very rock bottom level of old Downhill Street, was far and away the ugliest of the quartet, with nose twisted to one side, several knife scars cross-hatching the right cheek, the almost invisible eyes of a suspicious weasel. The irony was that Jim Joe considered himself uncommonly handsome and was known to erupt in offended rage should anyone suggest otherwise. Apart from this aberration, he was quietly efficient at what he did, which was much the same as his new companions. All three were small-time thugs, standover men and petty thieves.

The fourth man was the exception.

Telly Udo was the restless one in the corner. Smallest of the party yet by far the most menacing, he was a pale-faced dude with a shock of light-colored hair brushed straight back from a low forehead. Clean shaven and fastidiously neat in a tan belted jacket and striped stovepipe pants, Udo had been hired at a higher rate than the others as he was considered smarter, quicker with a gun and afraid of nothing, qualities which he might well be called upon to display when they finally rolled north up the Texas coast.

Or maybe that should be 'if', not 'when'. They had been waiting here a long time for Stein to get through across the road. Too long, maybe.

'Hey, sister?' Udo suddenly shouted as a couple strolled by, arm in arm. 'You lookin' to get laid tonight? Here I am.'

Instantly the muscular young man flushed with rage and lunged at the face in the coach window. A short chopping blow from Udo's .45 gun barrel broke his face open in a spray of hot crimson. The shocked girl filled her lungs to scream. Leaning from the window, Udo backhanded her hard, felling her to the sidewalk alongside her unconscious escort, her dress riding up over creamy thighs.

Udo laughed crazily as the whole street came sharply alert. Moments later the driver came rushing across from the Chicken House trailed by an angry Max Stein.

They were underway in moments before the first citizens could arrive on the scene. The Concord took a sharp corner on two wheels while Stein hung on tight and gave a grinning and relaxed Udo a strip of his tongue. The others were staring back. Nobody following. Not yet, leastways.

It was a long tense time before they began to relax, by which time they were deep in the raddled hills. Now sporadic conversations started up, everybody was glancing at Udo from the corner of their eyes then at Big Max, whose angry flush was finally beginning to fade. It was big Frick who finally put the question that had them all intrigued. Namely, wasn't it about time they were told what they'd been hired for?

'All in good time,' declared Max, a tall spare man who sported big black bushy sideburns and a black mustache in a failed attempt to appear Mexican.

'At least we oughta know where we're headed,' complained sombre Manny Clyde with an edge to his voice.

Max Stein hesitated as he glanced from face to face. Secrecy was the essence of this expedition, the planning of which had occupied him for almost a month. He did not want to reveal too much too soon yet by the same token felt it might be time to take them into his confidence, at least to a degree.

'Storm Bay,' he said casually. 'Ever heard of it?'

'Sounds like Hicksville,' commented Udo. 'So, what will we be doin' at this

Storm Bay, boss man?'

'For now, we'll call it a vacation.'

They stared at him disbelievingly but Stein had said all he was going to say. For now.

4

Badman From Mexico

Cord Mitchell slammed the final nail into the fence slat with a bang.

'That's in for life,' he stated, poker faced. 'In a thousand years' time, somebody will be digging in the ruins here and they are going to find that slat still nailed to that cross-beam.'

Jody studied him gravely until he saw the twinkle in his eye. Then he laughed and passed Cord more nails. He liked the way he talked at times like this, funny yet serious. He had stopped crying at night since the funeral.

Cord continued working on the collapsing fence in back of the stables where the chicken-run also stood in urgent need of repair. He wasn't quite sure how he'd started taking on odd jobs around the place. But he didn't worry about it any more than he did about his ongoing tenancy at the hotel. Sometimes in life it was just best to go with your instincts and not have to feel the need to examine everything under the microscope.

The morning stage from the north was in. Jinko was changing the horses and everyone else was at work inside. The banker had driven out from Bell's Landing the previous day in his gleaming sulky with a black documents-case tucked under his respectable arm. Cord sat in on the meeting with Connie to get a feel of what financial shape the place was really in. Turned out their situation was unhealthy but not yet critical. Unobserved, as the banker was leaving, Cord slipped him a hundred dollars on an outstanding note. The banker had confided that the late Thad Wheeler had not been a good manager, which hardly came as any shock.

The dog came by and tempted the boy away on some noisy game. Cord finished up with the section of fence and toted his tool kit across to the tack room, where he fashioned a cigarette while waiting for the coach to leave. It rolled right on by him, tall and swaying with the crew perched up on the high seat and well-fed passengers gazing out. Travellers invariably appeared in good spirits on quitting the hotel, something he attributed to good food and service. The hotel was a going concern but needed a financial boost right now, with winter drawing on and bookings already dropping off.

Cord grinned as he exhaled a cloud of white smoke. He was beginning to think like a businessman, he reflected wryly. He had never been that. Come to think on it, he had never been much of anything consistently, other than a gambling man incapable of staying put for long in any one place all his life; some kind of rebel on the drift. But it could well be he had played his last game, unless time could one day dim the memory of a shootout in Corpus

Christi, or sheer financial necessity drive him back to the tables.

He pondered reflectively on what it might be like to just stay in the one place doing the same work day after day, seeing the same faces, and most likely steering clear of trouble.

That life had plainly not suited Thad Wheeler; most likely it could never be for him either, he mused. An unwelcome thought that made him wonder if he and the dead man might not have been cut from the same cloth after all.

He realized Mary was calling from the dining-room door. He crossed the windy yard with his slouching relaxed stride to discover there was some gingerbread left over from the passengers' meal.

He sat at a long table with Joachim, still in his white cook's hat, as the woman bustled about clearing away.

The staff no longer subjected him to curious looks, he realized. Seemed as though he might be getting to be like part of the furniture, or at least accepted.

Joachim was rabbiting on about his cray-pots in the marsh when Connie came through from the kitchen. She nodded gravely; she was not an easy-smiling woman. Cord liked that. He supposed he liked most things about her. But he knew better than to show it. Even if he might feel almost welcome at the Thief Creek Hotel now, he was not prepared to risk putting it to the test with any show of over-familiarity.

She joined him as Joachim rose to go minister to the needs of his massive, clanking, iron range.

'I could see what you did to the fence from the kitchen window.' Connie broke a piece of ginger-bread in her fingers. 'I'm very grateful. But you really shouldn't, you know.'

'Ma'am,' he said, adopting an exaggerated drawl, 'this here is a free country and if a man with no calluses on his hands wants to go round pretending to be handyman then it's his constitutional right to make a fool of himself.'

She laughed. He had never heard her do that before. It stripped years from her. For a moment he saw the schoolgirl in her, fresh, untroubled and almost gay.

'You should do that more often,' he said.

'Would you like to see something to really laugh at?' she asked, serious again.

He nodded, and she led him from the room down the passageway to the office, where she produced a letter.

'The post office sent this out from Bell's with the stage,' she told him. 'He must have posted it yesterday, after visiting here and leading me on about our situation.'

It was from the banker. Following 'due consideration' of his discussion with Mrs Wheeler yesterday, the bank had reluctantly decided it could not extend their current note further than the end of the month. Yours faithfully, etc . . .

'Son of a . . . ' Cord began, but broke off. 'I thought we'd made an impression. Or you had, I mean.'

'I wasn't sure. I know how they think. 'No husband any more. How can a woman run a business like that?' Probably his dreary stick of a wife talked it over with him last night and told him he should move in on the mortgage before I run the place completely into the ground.'

'Look, I don't want to horn in on anything, but would you like me to ride in and see him? Beard the lion in its den sort of thing. I've talked lots of business with lots of people, shifty and otherwise. He's a stuffed shirt, but even they can be got around sometimes.'

'Why do I have this feeling you could do it, Cord?'

He shrugged. He both liked it when she looked at him that way, yet at the same time recoiled. It suggested a closeness that was impossible. There was a chasm between them, wide as a grave. A killing and a corpse. Any man with a lick of sense would have accepted that irrevocable fact of life and hightailed it from here long back.

They were chatting quietly when the peace of the day was abruptly shattered by Jody's voice as he came tearing across the yard, waving his hands, curls tossing in the wind.

'Mom, a coach just turned in off the trail. It's coming in.'

Everyone rose and went the windows. No coach was due until the next day. Jody informed his mother the rig had come up from the south.

'Probably someone who's just lost their way,' Connie speculated to Cord.

'Or then again it could be a coach full of paying guests,' he suggested facetiously.

Yet it turned out he was right when five passengers and a driver all seeking meals and accommodation rolled up to the doors with the brown-and-white hotel dog yapping at the teamers' heels.

They were tired businessmen from the south come to enjoy the peace and the fishing at backwater Storm Bay for a spell, they announced. They had cash and were ready to pay in advance. Even Cord was pleased the vacationers had shown up, while realizing immediately this would probably put period to his stay. He knew that deep down he had been waiting for the right moment to move on, as all loners must: some kind of diversion. He felt that Max 'Smith' and his party would provide just that.

* * *

Jody was sulking, nobody knew why.

The dog gave up trying to tempt the boy into a game of chasings and instead settled on the front porch with the wind gusts ruffling its hair, listening to the murmur of voices drifting from the windows.

The newly arrived guests had checked into their rooms and Mr Smith — the name Big Max chose to register under — was first to change into casual gear and come downstairs, where Connie was attending the desk, and the rattling coming from the kitchen indicated that supper would shortly be under way.

The man the others called simply 'Max' appeared relaxed as he thrust his hands into the hip pockets of Mexican charro trousers, which, like his bushy black sideburns and sweeping mustache, did not seem to fit with his all-American character and appearance.

The man was big, genial, confident. A critical eye might have detected something too large, tough and self-assured about this 'southern businessman', but no such intimations disturbed the proprietress as she energetically and happily brought her books up to date following the unexpected influx of patronage and cold hard cash. The party had paid for a week's full accommodation, in advance. This guaranteed Connie could easily meet the bank note this month, which augured well enough for the winter ahead.

Stein had taken over the hotel's best suite for himself upstairs, his associates settled in single rooms on the same floor.

With the wind blowing harder as it most often did with the approach of night, the lobby was warm and brightly lit as the tall man strolled across to the fireplace to lean a casual arm upon the fake marble mantel as Connie looked up.

'Coffee perhaps, or a drink?'

'Quite happy as I am at the moment, ma'am. Snug little place you have here.'

'Thank you. We like it.'

'Just you and your three staff, I take it?'

'Yes.'

'Mr Wheeler not here then?'

'My husband is recently deceased.'

'Oh, very sorry, ma'am. Shouldn't be so nosy. My wife always says that's one of my worst faults.'

'Oh, you're a family man then, Mr Smith?'

He smiled warmly, deep creases cutting his cheeks. 'Best little woman in the world, I'm happy to say. Mexican lady, as a matter of fact. Light of my life, as they say. Haven't seen her in quite some time but I hope to remedy that when I'm all through fishing.'

'You live in Mexico, then?'

'Oh, you mean the way I dress and suchlike. Matter of fact I do, Mrs Wheeler. Visited down there some years back and just 'went Mex', as the expression goes. Loved the place and stayed in love with it when I married my bride. Great country if you like chilli, as they say. So. Manny, how you settling in, boy?'

Manny Clyde came down the stairs in his quiet way, nodded politely to the woman and drifted across to the sofa.

'Just fine, Max. Wind's a bit of a bother though.'

Max smiled genially across at Connie.

'Manny's an inlander. Can't get used to the coast. Hails from the stone hills and scrub hollows and hard scrabble ranches of West Texas, so he does. Hell of a flytaster though, aren't you, pard?'

'Right,' Clyde grunted, taking a seat. 'Where are the others?'

'Well,' said Max, 'if I know Jim Joe he'd be looking to stretch out and catch forty winks before supper, and Frick would be still unpacking.' He shrugged. 'Telly? Who knows? Nobody knows what Telly might do next, including Telly.'

'That's Mr Udo you're referring to, I take it?' asked Connie. They nodded, and she went on. 'Are you all five up from Mexico then, gentlemen?'

'Only me, ma'am,' Max said in a way that seemed to close off that line of discussion. He began circling the room, checking the pictures and photographs, and Connie thought he moved more fluently and athletically than most men of his age and occupation. He was down in the register as an importer. He gave the impression he would not be comfortable behind a desk. 'My buddies are all too young, too foolish and footloose to take a bride and settle down, I'm sorry to say.'

Bootheels sounded above. The bulky Frick and Jim Joe Jackson came down together to join Manny Clyde on the sofas by the north windows. When a small face showed at the porch windows, Frick turned his big head sharply, then grinned.

'Just the kid.' He beckoned. 'Come on in and visit, kid. We won't bite.'

The face vanished and did not reappear. Jody was crossing the blustery yard, kicking at leaves and pouting again as he made for the stables.

He searched around for Cord. The two had become fast friends and Jody was dreading the day the tall man saddled up and left. Cord had been everyplace and told him stories of cities and sailing round Cape Horn in something called a 'windjammer'. In the hotel tack-room he had shown him how to make bullets out of bar lead.

Just having Cord around seemed to help everyone feel better about what had happened to his father, Jody felt. Especially himself. He could tell his mother liked him also by the way she always poured him an extra cup of coffee at table. Other things too.

He'd never known a guest to pitch in and help with the chores, yet it seemed natural for Cord to do so. He would bet none of these new guests would help out any. And wondered why he seemed to be the only one who didn't like them.

Sometimes Joachim's strange woman told the boy he showed quite a gift for reading people, a talent for which, among others, she herself was renowned. Jody was not sure what that meant, although he always knew immediately whom he liked or didn't. He didn't like these men from the South and it was because of this that he was now making for the stables to look over their horses and gear while trying to figure out just why he should feel that way about them. He'd hated and feared his own father, something he felt vaguely guilty about now he was dead and gone.

Back in the front room, Joachim appeared in the doorway, wiping flour from his hands on his apron, to announce supper would be ready shortly. Frick and Clyde ordered drinks, which Joachim passed on to Jinko.

'Brazos River fish fry,' stated the cook-cum-handyman-cum-Jack-of-all-trades. 'Catfish, eggs half-beaten, salt, chilli powder, pepper and oatmeal. How's that sound?'

'Sounds like something you'd pizen a goat with, brother.'

Telly Udo was descending from the upper level, scrubbed, clean-shaven and trim as a dancer in snug-fitting Levis and black shirt. Unlike the others, who appeared to be unarmed, the fair-headed Texan with the unnerving laugh and too-bright eyes wore a double gunrig with two Colt holsters thonged to slim thighs.

Max frowned at sight of the hardware

but did not comment. Joachim was also scowling, but Udo just giggled and made a placatory gesture.

'Just kidding, brother. Sounds great. Heck, sounds almost good enough to eat, hey, hey.' He flung his arms wide. 'And here he is, I do declare. What you got there? Looks like oysters.'

Cord came in through the side door and closed it behind him. A hessian sack heavy with oyster-shells hung from his hand. He'd gone off alone to the marsh after the newcomers' arrival to return anything but empty-handed.

'Evening,' he greeted, coming deeper into the room. He wore rough gear from the marsh and his dark hair was tousled from the wind. Connie watched him as he passed his haul to a beaming Joachim, and Max Stein thoughtfully studied them both.

For reasons nobody at Storm Bay could begin to guess, it was very important to Max that he find out as much as possible about the personnel and the operation of the Thief Creek

Hotel as he waited either for his fish to start biting, or for something else entirely different.

'You must like weather to be out there on a night like this, Mitchell,' he remarked in a personable way. 'Or maybe it's just that I've gotten too soft, hunched over a damned desk. You might want to show us the best fishing spots tomorrow?'

Cord was glancing across at Connie now.

'I'm not sure I'll still be here,' he said quietly.

Again Max was quick to note the woman's reaction. Her eyes widened and her lips compressed, showing quite clearly that this announcement came as an unpleasant surprise. Yet she said nothing and Cord turned his attention back to Max.

'You'll most likely have to fish from the rocks or the jetties. We don't have a boat big enough to take out on this water.'

'To tell you the God's honest truth,'

replied Max, 'I don't much care if we catch anything or not. What's appealing about being here for the rest of the week is the peace and quiet. Isn't that so, boys?'

Four heads nodded. Seemed to Cord Mitchell that importer Smith liked being surrounded by yes-men. But hard men also, if he was any judge, and he surely was. His gaze drifted across to Udo, and he felt the impact of level blue eyes like a touch of frost. A sensation of vague disquiet stirred him, but he was quick to thrust it to one side. It's time, Mitchell, he reminded himself. Time to get riding . . . and don't go looking for fake reasons to stay on.

Mary called from the kitchen and Joachim ushered the party down the short connecting passageway to leave Cord and Connie momentarily alone.

'I didn't know you were leaving,' she complained. 'Why? You don't have anything special to do, do you?'

'What makes you think that?' he

replied, moving to lean an elbow on the desk. He smelt of wind and seaspray and the marsh, and the woman was aware of it.

'Well, reading between the lines on what you've said about yourself, Mr Mitchell, you are not tied down by responsibilities or duties, are you? So if you have noplace particular to go, why not stay here a little longer?'

He had heaps of reasons including guilt, and an increasing sense of unease whenever alone in the company of Connie Wheeler, like now.

Was it even remotely possible, that in the brief time they had known one another they had become almost close — the way strangers might do when drawn together by some disaster?

At similar times in the past, at the first hint of genuine closeness, Cord Mitchell had found that more than enough reason to saddle and ride. He was considering doing this again, yet he found the decision to cut and run unconscionably difficult for some reason.

He'd killed this woman's husband and had not confessed to it, and this was why he could feel the trail calling. Get gone before she found out. Or they, rather. Mother and son. They'd both want to see him fry when they learned the truth of Wheeler's death and he did not want to be around to see something genuinely good and unexpected in his life turn ugly.

'I'll think it over,' he said off-handedly. 'Shall we go in?'

She brushed back her dark hair with her hands. She wore no face powder or lip rouge. She didn't need it. Looked like a real woman. Made a long succession of saloon chippies, prissy young ladies with wealthy parents, or modern emancipated beauties on the hunt for husbands and fine homes look pretty insipid and shallow by compari-son. Might as well face it. He liked her a great deal. Did he need any better reason to take off than that?

At that moment Jody burst through the porch door looking wide-eyed and excited.

'Mom, Cord,' he panted as the dog forced its way in before he could get the door closed again. 'There's a bag of guns hidden in the barn, I just seen them.'

'Saw,' Connie corrected automatically, frowning. 'There are no weapons in the stables, Jody.'

'Sure there are.' He pointed towards the dining-room. 'They brought them with them, stashed them in the loft. Rifles and sixshooters and lots of bullets. You want to come see, Cord?'

'Of course he doesn't,' Connie answered for him. She paused, then went on, 'In any case, if they have rifles then I'm sure that's their business. They are on vacation after all. They probably hope to go hunting as well as fishing.'

'Then why hide them?' Cord found himself pondering out loud.

'Supper will be growing cold,' Connie said severely. Dutifully the tall man and the small boy followed her tall figure down the passageway.

★   ★   ★

The armour-plated prison coach stood squat and ready before the Harlingen law office as Marshal Prade emerged, drawing on his gloves. The marshal was a spit-and-polish peace officer of the old school with no sense of humor and an enviable record in the Service. By contrast, Junior Marshal Hanline was laconic, sometimes witty, had not been in the marshal's office long enough to acquire too many citations or reputation. Even so, the youthful towhead with the ready grin had done enough in a couple of testing assignments of late to attract the attention of Prade, who had subsequently floated his name when organizing the transportation north to Corpus Christi from the Rio Grande of one Lino Guardia, late of Old Mexico.

'You've checked out everything as

instructed, Hanline?'

'Yes, sir. Inspected the wagon, double-checked the team, tested the locks and security devices. The driver and look-out are ready and waiting, as you can see, so all we seem to need now is our prisoner.'

'Indeed,' replied the starchy Prade, linking gloved hands behind his back and glancing towards the lock-up. 'Señor Lino Guardia,' he intoned with some satisfaction. 'Some kind of foolish folk-hero across the border, or so they say, but in the sovereign state of Texas, proven brigand, bandit, train-wrecker and probably murderer. We should be honored to be awarded the responsibility of escorting such a notoriety to Corpus Christi, and the hangman, don't you agree, Hanline?'

'Certainly, sir.' It was Hanline's first major job and he was taking it seriously. He frowned. 'But do you really believe he will be hanged?'

'If there is such a thing as Texas justice, no question about it.'

Hanline frowned.

'But surely there is some doubt about Guardia's venality, Marshal Prade. They say he's some kind of folk-hero down in San Bonito, although I'll concede that's far from the case this side of the border. Yet I'm sure you'll agree he has a very soft reputation compared to the real villains and desperadoes Mexico produces. And don't you consider it extraordinary that such a man should enjoy such a high reputation in his native land and apparently confine all his robbing and pillaging — allegedly on behalf of the poor — to Texas?'

'What I believe, sir,' Prade said testily, 'is that the Mexican authorities choose to turn a blind eye to this felon's depredations simply to cover the fact that they can never succeed in laying hands upon him, and because of his vast popularity with the masses. This could never prevail in Texas, and it's significant that it was the skills of the marshals and the Texas Rangers that yet again proved to be so superior to those of our southern counterparts when they captured the rogue trying to cross the Rio. And now we have this Texas-hating felon in our hands we shall see him justly hanged, you may be sure of that.'

Hanline nodded. He understood. He threw a snappy salute.

'Permission to remove prisoner from his cell and place him aboard the van, sir.'

'Granted.'

When Señor Lino Guardia was led blinking and manacled from his dark cell he didn't look much like the popular conception of a swashbuckling Mexican folk-hero or notorious Texas bank-robber. Short and bow-legged with a toothy grin which seemed fixed in place, he looked more like some petty thief whose hand you might suddenly feel rummaging in your jacket pocket, than a swashbuckler of considerable notoriety whose last widely publicized endeavor below the Rio had been to lead a raid upon the infamous

Los Santos Penitentiary to free a supposedly innocent friend. It seemed that this hair-raising piece of bravado on Guardia's part had been largely ignored by the Mexican authorities for the unlikely reason that they regarded both Los Santos prison and indeed all the *Regulare*-controlled Castillo Valley as a hotbed of quasi-lawful corruption and crime which deserved everything it got. But officially recognized or not, the outraged *Regulares* had pursued Guardia remorselessly all the way from the valley to the Rio, which he was swimming on his horse and making vulgar gestures back at his chagrined pursuers when a squad of Texas Rangers popped out of the tall reeds on the American shore to nab, hogtie, jug and bottle him with enormous relish.

If the genuine Mexican authorities — as opposed to Castillo Valley's corrupt *Regulares* regime — didn't want this man, then Austin certainly did.

Get Guardia!

This had been a daunting challenge for Lone Star law ever since toothily-grinning Lino, so highly regarded as a man of the people and enemy of oppression in San Cristobal, had first jumped the border to do battle with the lawmen of Texas and Los Estados Unitos. Since then Guardia's depredations north of the Rio had increased seemingly in direct ratio to his ever increasing popularity back home.

His crimes against the Lone Star banking companies were many and varied, but it was the most recent of these which was responsible for him finding himself grinning here in the torch-light and blinking up at an armoured prison-van in Harlingen tonight. Two months previously, irrepressible Guardia had plundered the bank in Kingsville and returned to Mexico with several thousand dollars in American currency which, so it was reliably reported, he had promptly donated to the 'shirtless ones of

Catarina Province', drawing *olés!*'
down south while lifting Texan fury to
white heat up north.

US law was determined to have its
day in court with Señor Lino Guardia,
and despite mild and totally unprofes-
sional protests from the Mexican
authorities, he would shortly be *en
route* north tonight to face judge and
jury in Kingsville.

'Why are you grinning like an ape?'
Prade expected people in custody to
conduct themselves with nothing less
than respectful gravity.

'Such a velvet night, Señor Marshal,'
came the gentle reply. 'Lino is simply
happy to be still alive.' Then he had to
add, 'And in such splendid company!'

Prade hated Mexicans. He was
honest about it. They were too casual,
happy, frivolous and lacking in respect
for his tastes. And yet behind the
marshal's tight-lipped visage, tonight
there lurked a sneaking hint of admira-
tion for this rogue, for Lino Guardia
was the rarest of all wrongdoers here in

the turbulent south-east corner.

A Robin Hood.

The marshal knew for a fact that Guardia loved the poor and lavished whatever he could steal upon them. That he was a genuine *caballero* who hated the tax-gatherers, apparently had no interest in personal advancement or grandeur, and whose name was revered by every Mexican with holes in his britches and many others besides.

Quite possibly they would hang him for the bank job, but Prade still had almost to admire the fellow — despite that annoying smile.

'All right, load him up,' he ordered officiously.

As Prade stepped back to watch the procedure a small group of local law officials stood by, taking their last look at the man who had been their prisoner for some time now. These men were relieved to see him go as there were constant rumors that attempts might be made to break Guardia out of their lock-up here, just as he had done in

Mexico recently when he led that attack upon the crumbling Los Santos penitentiary to free an inmate.

The pimply-faced law office clerk with the big nose and furtive expression was unnoticed in the group, his expression studiedly neutral as steel doors slammed on Lino Guardia and the huge padlock locked securely. There was nothing remarkable about this youth other than that in this tightly knit group of Harlingen peace officers he was the only one who could be bribed.

One week earlier, not far from this very spot in the heart of the river cattle country, and for a considerable sum of money, this clerk had revealed to Max Stein that the schedule for Guardia's transport from Harlingen to Kingsville had his escort party booked in ahead to overnight at the Thief Creek Hotel at Storm Bay.

5

Deep Water Night

'Crack them, swallow them, crack another,' advised Joachim. 'There's an old saying along the coast that if a man eats a dozen oysters a day he'll live to a hundred and sire a hundred children.'

Cord tilted his head back to swallow down a fat Owl Marsh oyster. Times like this a man needed no further proof that there really was a God.

'So,' he said, 'how come you haven't reproduced by this?'

'Because I'm old, ugly and much reduced by a misspent youth. But with a fellow like you it's a different matter entirely. You're young, full of juice, and women like the cut of your rig. You should be a daddy a dozen times over by this.'

They stood knee-deep in surging water with a bulging reedy hummock in back of them and dark cloud-masses surging across the face of a cold moon.

Joachim's excuse for accompanying Mitchell on his nocturnal excursion around the southern curve of the bay was to ensure the 'tenderfoot' didn't fall into a slew, never to be sighted again.

Cord sensed there was more to it than this, yet was pretty certain that potency, or the lack of it, was definitely not it.

He attempted a change of subject.

'Those house guests back at the hotel, they seem — '

'Miz Connie's a very lonely woman these days,' the big brown man overrode with a meaningful sideways glance.

Cord felt vaguely offended.

'What does that have to do with me?'

'She reckons you're handsome.'

He studied the man narrowly. 'And I reckon you're full of buffalo-dust.'

'So, you're not really interested, is that it?'

'Look, you're starting to strain a friendship. You're talking about a woman who's just lost her husband — '

'Who she didn't love and who treated her and the kid badly.'

' — and I'm just passing by,' Cord continued as though the other had not spoken. He indicated a distant bobbing light across the bay. 'Like that ship yonder.'

The vessel seemed scarcely to move against the tide. It was a tugboat, pushing three barges of clam-shells up the channel. It sounded its horn, muffled and mournful. This really was a long way from the wide Texas range-lands Mitchell knew best. Joachim cracked and swallowed a final oyster before replying.

'I worry about Miz Connie, always did.' He jerked his head in the direction of Jagged Spur, beyond which the crouched shape of the hotel was dimly visible. 'Times like now more than most . . .'

Cord sensed his chance and took it. 'You mean Smith and his crew?'

Joachim nodded, indicating they should move on. The currents tugged strongly at their legs. They were rugged up against the chill. Underfoot, marine things crackled, crunched and grunted. It was cold, clean and good to be prowling the marsh at night, refreshingly different from the hotel from which they had departed an hour before.

'Strange bunch that,' Joachim commented. 'Wrong time of year, wrong look for vacationers. They are polite enough, and they have paid ahead, always a good sign. Smith seems OK if a little cross-grained. But the others are . . . well, what do you make of the others, Mr Mitchell?'

Cord didn't answer immediately. He was parading the other four through his mind, setting each man beneath the microscope.

Frick resembled a gorilla in a vast coat, customcut especially to fit. Jackson was ugly enough to make a warthog look good, but by contrast sober and somber Manny Clyde looked like Mr Average from Noplace. That this trio might be shifty, even shady, there now seemed to be little doubt. Yet if hardcase was indeed their brand they were easy enough to get along with. They were polite to Connie and the others, played along with Jody, yet he still believed they might be about twice as tough as they acted.

Then there was Udo.

He frowned and couldn't help it. He was ready to wager the full roll he was packing that Telly Udo was the real thing — crooked, vicious, desperado, gun-punk. He'd encountered that breed from Amarillo to the Pecos, and you couldn't miss them. They might as well go round wearing a big sign reading; WARNING — DANGER!

He nodded to himself. No doubt about it, Udo was the one that made a man uneasy. Yet then he had to ask himself, so what? He was nobody's keeper, certainly had no right or authority to question people on the quality of guest they allowed to sashay through their hotel doors.

And he realized belatedly that, subconsciously, he had wanted to draw Joachim away from the hotel now in the hope that the man might reassure him about the guests, to set his mind at rest, even though they were really none of his concern anyway.

Finally he put his question straight, and Joachim answered in the same vein as they rounded an island and raised a muted light across a narrow channel.

'To tell you the truth, they all bother me, Mr Mitchell. As I say, Smith seems OK, yet there's even somethin' about him that doesn't set right. That man is on edge. And he is harder than he looks. I've heard him talking to the others when he thought there was nobody about. He claims they are business associates yet he talks to them like hired help. He doesn't carry, but all the others do. That giggling Udo dresses and struts like a genuine pistoleer. I can tell you this, I would feel a whole lot better about this situation if you weren't aimin' to quit.'

Cord halted abruptly.

'Who said I'm leaving?'

Joachim stopped and stared at him levelly. 'Tell me you're not, then.'

Cord was silent. For it was true. Joachim and Crow Woman were hard folks to fool. He was indeed ready to check out. Had been even before the party's arrival. Moving on before things got too complicated — whatever he might mean by that.

'Silence says it all, I reckon.' Joachim sighed, moving on across the channel. 'Well, it's a free country and you are a free agent. It's just that . . . '

The wind snatched his words away. Cord drew abreast, thick coarse hair tossing wildly.

'Well, go on, say it,' he panted. 'What?'

'Just thought the way fate brought you here, and the way you hit it off with all of us — which is pretty unusual in itself — that you might have got the notion of puttin' down roots. I mean, it's not as if you got family, friends or business waiting you anyplace, is it? You've levelled with me and I appreciate it, Mr Mitchell. And you've made it crystal clear to me that you are a man without roots, while at the same time settin' the notion buzzin' away in my head that you might be feelin' that roots are the very thing in life you're missin'.'

'Want a word of advice, Joe?'

'Sure.'

'Stick to cooking and leave the backwoods philosophizing to those better suited to it.' Cord pointed. 'That your woman I can see yonder?'

The houseboat loomed ahead. Joachim sighed and nodded. His houseboat and his woman right enough. 'We'll have some coffee before headin' back. Pot's never off the stove at my place.'

'You're going back to the hotel tonight? Why?'

'You know why, Mr Mitchell. You just

don't want to own to the fact that you're as worried as I am. We'll put our catch in the boathouse first. 'Night, darlin'!' he called. Then softly, 'Good woman. Good with a knife. So good with a knife in truth that any man livin' under the same roof would be six kinds of a fool not to treat her right. You could wake up one mornin' and find crawfish feedin' off your head in the channel.'

Cord had to smile. The boathouse was small and square, set up on empty oil drums. With the water down, the drums had settled into the mud, canting it slightly to one side. There was a single-plank wharf with two boats tied to a pylon. Both boats sat in the mud. They stashed their sacks in the building, then walked along the sloping blanks to reach the houseboat, where rich coffee aromas filled the air.

Somehow it irked Cord to find himself totally at ease and relaxed over the following hour as they sat around smoking, sipping great joe and talking like old friends.

It was almost as though there was a conspiracy afoot to convince Cord Mitchell that this was about the safest safe harbor he'd ever entered, that Storm Bay and everyone on it and everything beneath it would be just tickled pink if he should simply admit to this fact and announce his intention of renouncing his life as a free spirit and set down roots. They would wait a long time.

For it was not that he never had been or would be the settling kind. There was also his secret. Too late to blurt it out now. He'd passed that point of no return days ago. The time must surely come, maybe sooner than he knew, when the secret of Wheeler's death finally surfaced like a drowned corpse. He intended being long gone when that happened. Could live without seeing Connie's and the boy's warmth towards him turn to ice. If this made him a coward, so be it. He was not usually as considerate of other people as this, and that in itself was just one more upright reason to hit leather and ride, maybe as soon as tonight.

The woman returned from the stove with what Cord vowed must be his last mug of 'Joachim coffee' which was regular Owl Marsh coffee comprising grounds, half coffee and half brandy.

Crow Woman smiled at him as she handed him his mug. She was short and heavy. She wore a flowered skirt and dark cloth jacket. Her coal-black hair was tied back from her broad face with a green ribbon. At that very moment, close members of her tribal family were burning down a rancher's spread by the light of a Llano Estacado moon. She kissed the top of Joachim's head then fetched him a big old dragoon's model Colt to carry back to the hotel on his hip. She too sensed something in the air, and she had the advantage of access to gopher entrails, readings, and words of warning written by snakes wriggling in the sand to support her avowed clairvoyance.

Cord really felt like he was saying goodbye to something valuable when eventually he left, and trudging around the shoreline below the spur with Joachim striding along at his side with a long staff in his hand and his Colt thrusting from his belt, he was feeling the liquor some yet was still fully alert as ever.

It was he who spotted the figure first. The man was outlined against the tattered night sky atop the spur. As they stopped and gazed upwards they realized it was Big Max Smith, staring out to see beyond the headland, greatcoat flapping in the wind behind him.

'Strange,' Joachim muttered as they moved on. 'Didn't I say they were?'

'What's strange about coming to the sea and enjoying it? Isn't that what they are paying for?'

'People just don't come to the seaside in winter.'

'I'm here, aren't I?'

They walked on, leaning against that

wind. Behind them in the night Max Stein continued to stare out towards the Gulf so intently he was not even aware of them passing by below.

★ ★ ★

Telly Udo stood at the far end of the diner's longest table, leaning against the servery counter with his slender back rested against the leading edge and one bootheel hooked on to the footrail.

'Not a smart idea,' Manny Clyde was opining from his place at another table where he sat fashioning a cigarette. 'Max wouldn't want you doin' anythin' like that without his say-so, without his bein' here. No sir.'

'Crap.'

Udo tilted his head back to stare at the ceiling. Then he leant forward to glance along the short passageway leading to the foyer, which he had seen Mitchell and Joachim enter from outside several minutes earlier.

'Mitchell's gotta go,' he continued,

keeping his voice low. 'We know it, Max knows it, but he's still here. Time we handed him his ticket. Here, buster, take this and use it. Don't forget to write. Piss off.'

Frick stirred ponderously as he sat hunched over a hot toddy by a dark window. Although all had been recruited in Diamondback, they were still merely acquaintances, not pards. And yet some kind of camaraderie was beginning to jell between Frick, Jackson and Clyde from which Telly Udo was excluded. Indeed it could well be Udo who was pushing them together. The trio were tough enough, but none cared for Udo, indeed were increasingly wary of the man ever since his cold-blooded killing for no reason back in Harlingen, which had earned their caution along with their grudging respect.

How Max felt about the grinning guntipper was not known. He kept his own counsel. Yet Max was *numero uno*, and here was Udo acting as though he believed that in the big man's absence he could call the shots.

'We are supposed to be businessmen on vacation, Udo,' the giant reminded. 'Remember? We don't raise dust and we don't go pushin' other guests around. Right now, that's what Max is payin' us to do.'

'There's something real fishy about Mitchell,' Udo persisted. He indicated their surroundings. 'He doesn't fit. See the way he wears a gun? How quick his hands move when he's workin' on something? This geezer smells of city smoke. He's smooth and he knows what fork to use, yet he's got a real hard eye when he puts it on a man. We're told he just stopped off here to bring the woman some bad news. But how come he's still here? Couldn't be anything to do with our business by any chance. Or could it?'

'You're forgettin' something, ain't you?' Jackson queried.

'Such as?'

'We don't know what our business is ourselves yet.'

Udo pushed away from the bar, brimful of restless energy, a man always riding an edge. 'That's another thing I don't cotton to,' he protested. 'All this hush-hush stuff. What's so hairy about Max's business here that he can't tell his own hired hands what brand goes on what steer's hairy ass? Anyway, all we can be certain of is that he didn't handpick a bunch of dab gunhands like us to help him catch crawfish or bring down the odd squirrel for supper.'

Cold blue eyes raked his audience as he paused.

'Only a dumb player will go into a game where he doesn't know the rules. That's us. And we're in this game because we couldn't resist the dough. But if Max is fixing to throw us into action somewhere along the line here, I don't want a joker in the deck like Mitchell around when it happens. That is just asking for trouble. So I say it again, he's got to go.' They stared at him thoughtfully now.

Udo returned their looks with an

arrogant lift to his chin.

They still did not care for him, but could no longer deny he was making sense.

'Figured you'd see it my way in the end,' he smirked and was on his way, stepping lightly down the hallway, radiating eagerness in every step.

'We back his play?' muttered Frick.

'It's his deal, let him play it out,' responded Manny Clyde. 'We might buy in if it gets serious.'

Seated in the lobby enjoying what he intended to be his last cigarette of the day, Cord heard the steps in the passageway and the murmur of voices in the dining-room but took little notice. He was sipping a gin, which might or might not be his last, and was poised to come to a decision on his immediate future.

Go or stay?

It must be go, insisted the sober half of his brain while the other half had other ideas.

The sudden appearance of the

snake-hipped gunman helped focus his thinking remarkably. In an instant he was sharper, keener, less alcohol-affected. In poker games, a man never sat with his back to a man who looked like Telly Udo.

'Still here, Mitchell?'

'Looks like it.'

'Been crawfishing again?'

'Something like that.'

'Crawfishing by night, odd jobbing by day . . . ' Udo sauntered across to lean an elbow on the desktop. 'Just a knockabout, roustabout kind of guy, huh?'

'Is there a point to this?' Cord said, rising smoothly.

'With me there's always a point. The point with you is that you're no more a handyman or oyster farmer than I am. You are an operator, Mitchell, and your breed makes my breed nervous.' A quick empty smile. 'That's why you're leaving. I could say this hotel ain't big enough for both of us, but I won't. All I'm saying is, *adios*.'

For a short space it was still.

Cord's fingertips tingled and a familiar cool calm was washing through him. He'd been down this road before, read all the signs, understood the hazards. This was not a thinking man's situation. Such a man would immediately put on his hat and leave, for Telly Udo's every word and gesture was a warning you could not deny. Cord chose to stand his ground. At such times the quiet man in him stepped aside and the seasoned veteran of a thousand saloon face-downs took over. This Cord Mitchell was basically not such a far cry from Udo himself insofar as nobody got to tell him what to do. Not ever.

Setting his drink aside he hooked his thumb in his shell belt above his Colt.

Telly Udo looked a little startled as he moved back a pace. He read all the danger signs; he simply had not expected Cord's reaction to be so challenging.

'You are making a big mistake, big

man,' he said with a sudden suppressed laugh. He snorted. 'Biggest mistake of your crummy life, in truth.' He was deliberately working himself up. 'I offered you a fair break, you turned down my offer, so now we are going to have to find us another way . . . '

The creaking of a door caused Udo to spin swiftly. Connie Wheeler came through from her office, her face pale but unflinching as she took in a scene that even a blind man could interpret accurately. Yet her voice was calm.

'Sorry if I'm interrupting anything. Mr Udo, Joachim is taking a nightcap into the diner for you and your friends — '

'Go straight to hell, sister,' Udo almost shouted, not taking his eyes off Cord now. 'Go . . . go wash your dishes why don't you? Your boyfriend and me have got some business that just won't wait. Ain't that so — big man?'

'Do as he says,' Cord warned.

'I'm not leaving.' Connie's voice trembled now. 'I don't know what this is about but I — '

'Shut up, you stupid bitch!' Udo was shaking with irrational fury. 'Go, stay, suck eggs or lay 'em, just shut your stupid mouth, sister. Now, drifter, we've come to it and I'm going to sack your saddle for no better reason than that you couldn't take a hint. Go for iron and pray!'

Before Cord could respond there came a heavy clatter of steps from the porch and Max Stein lunged into the room boosted by a big gust of wind.

'Cut it!' he barked instantly, swinging across the lobby, his focus on the twisted, pinched face of his hired hitman. Halting before Udo, towering over him, he jerked a thumb in the direction of the dining-room. 'Whatever is going on here I don't want to know about it. I'll see you later, Telly.'

'But, Max, you don't understand.'

'Did you hear what I said?'

To the watching Cord, it was a moment which could have gone either way, and he was ready whichever way the dice should roll. There could be no doubting that Udo was white-hot mad clear through, and still of a mind to escalate nothing into gunsmoke. But Max was dominating him with the power of his personality. You could see it working. And when the other three appeared at the dining-room entrance to stare out at them, Udo finally dropped his eyes, twisted his lips and actually stamped his heel on the boards before swinging violently away.

It was this show of childish, almost feminine petulance that lent the scene its final touch of the bizarre. The confrontation seemed to have come out of nothing yet must certainly have led to bloodshed but for the timing of Stein's intervention.

Even Max himself appeared a little shaken as Udo flung through the doors into the night and Frick, Jackson and Clyde turned back for the diner.

'Thank you, Mr Smith,' Connie said simply.

'My regrets, ma'am,' Stein responded.

He turned to Cord, who'd picked up his glass and was taking a pull on it. He couldn't help but note the rock steadiness of his hand or the way he looked so calm when Stein sensed he was not. 'And to you too, Mitchell. It won't happen again.'

'How can you be sure?' Cord asked.

Max appeared almost preoccupied. 'Huh? What do you mean?'

'He's a mad dog as anyone can see. Who can control one?'

'Ah, Telly's bark's worse than his bite,' stated Max, carrying the canine analogy through. He was making for the diner, and Cord was recalling him as he had sighted him all alone atop the spur, staring out at the Gulf like a tall sea captain. 'Boys!' he called. 'Your boss needs a drink.'

Cord let a long handful of seconds slide by before tipping his glass to his lips and draining it. He was forcing the incident from his mind and focusing on the decision he had made, what must now be said.

'Connie — ' he began, but got no farther.

'I have an idea what you're going to say, Cord,' she interrupted. 'But I wish you would hear what I wish to say first.' He grimaced. Saying goodbye was going to prove even harder than he'd expected, and he didn't want to delay it. But then he finally met her eyes, and that was a big mistake.

'Sure,' he heard himself say. 'Say away.'

★   ★   ★

Too late to quit now.

So ran Max Stein's weighty thoughts as he stood by his window staring out at the yards, the trees and the trace of the Gilmour Trail to the hotel, down which Lino would soon be arriving.

With every passing day he was made more aware just how much of the old edge his years of peaceful living had cost him. He could still cut it, of course, but he had to work at it, while his judgement, once so canny and sure, was now suspect.

Maybe he'd made a huge impulsive mistake in setting out to save Lino in return for his having saved him, he mused. He had certainly made a major error in hiring Udo, who was getting harder to control every hour. But he couldn't quit now. All Texas was sore at Lino, which wasn't the same thing as having enough evidence to hang him. But hang him they would if his brother-in-law didn't snatch him from the jaws of the marshals, just as Caballero had snatched him from Los Santos.

He nodded somberly, knowing he would never quit. Not now. With name, honor and family pride all at stake, Big Max was riding a train he couldn't get off.

6

Los Santos and Lino

*When you set aside the cards and
  take up the gun
There's just no tellin' how your
  luck's gonna run . . .*

Cord Mitchell was sore. Turned out Joachim had forewarned Connie of his intentions to quit. Thanks a bunch, Joe! Now Connie was pressing him to stay on, perhaps even at a reduced rate; they could discuss that later. Claimed she appreciated the good effect he appeared to be having on her son about whom she had become increasingly concerned following the loss of his father. When Cord showed stubborn she used his own words against him, and he couldn't deny he'd told them he had no specific destination in mind in his journey south. Connie then used this point to emphasize the contrast between simply drifting on aimlessly and staying on at Storm Bay, perhaps even until the weather improved.

Cord sat in her cramped office with yet another glass in his fist as the wind-gusts hit the weatherboards and somewhere a shutter began to rattle. Drinking too much again. This wasn't really his style, but then neither was allowing himself to get involved with people. That was a loner's no-no. The longer Connie Wheeler spoke the more sense she made, and the worse he felt. And wondered again: why in hell had he not told them all the truth on day one, then he wouldn't be in this position now.

He was only half-listening as she went on:

'You say you like to gamble and do deals, whatever that may mean. Well, you could do all that in Bell's Landing but make your base here. You see, I think you've brought us luck, Cord. First there was Mr Smith's party, and then tomorrow we're expecting more guests to overnight with us. We're never this busy this time of year — '

'I can't stay.' The liquor was thickening his tongue a little but his words were all too clear. And brusque, he was sure. But he couldn't help it. This was running time and Cord Mitchell was poised for flight.

How could he have expected the body blow she delivered while he was rising from his chair?

'This may be the most foolish thing I've ever said,' Connie declared, looking down at her locked hands on the desk. 'But I have to tell you I've grown quite fond of you, Cord.'

There it was. Straight right to the heart. Almost took his breath away, and naturally made him feel like a Grade A son of a bitch.

'Connie . . . '

'No, please let me finish.' Now she looked up at him directly. 'I was aware of it that first day you rode in with the terrible news. The attraction, I mean. I know it must sound awful, probably is. But the fact is that my marriage to Thad had become a sham a long time ago. And you just seemed so . . . so different in every way, strong, reliable . . . '

'And a fraud,' he cut in bitterly. No stopping it now. Now it had to come out before she could say any more to make him feel even worse. 'I'm sorry, Connie,' he blurted, snatching up his hat, 'but if you made a mistake with your husband it was nothing to the mistake you're making about me. You see, it was me who killed him at Corpus Christi. Shot him in a fight over a poker game. That's why I felt I had a duty to come here and tell you and face the music. Only I didn't expect . . . expect . . . '

He couldn't face her now; he flung violently from the room. Connie cried out his name but he was jogging stiff-legged and unsteady to reach the hitch rail and throw himself into the saddle. Dizzy from emotion, hard liquor and some kind of bitter relief that the ugly truth was finally out, Cord Mitchell found himself pounding the Bell's Landing trail before the next big blow came across the water, the sound in the trees like a woman weeping.

★ ★ ★

The fishing-boat pitched in the swell as it continued its way up the darkened coastline. Miguel the fisherman could never sleep or eat comfortably without a bucking deck beneath his boots, but for his sister it was different. Evalina had not been to sea since brothers and sister had gone out with their father's fleet from San Bonito many years earlier. She had still managed to find her sea legs to a degree as the *Rafaela* beat its way northwards from Mexican waters this journey, but was still far from comfortable. But Evalina as always was the woman of great spirit and refused to complain of the queasiness and backache which were in reality as much attributable to her condition as to the pitch and toss of the sturdy *Rafaela*. On this leg of the journey she'd even insisted on taking the tiller to relieve her brother who now sat in the stern behind the wheelhouse, smoking his foul black pipe and watching the forbidding coastline of Texas slide by to the west.

This coastline intimidated Captain Miguel because he was far outside Mexican waters, was engaged in something highly illegal on this secret journey, and had every good reason to fear the stern gentlemen of the gringo coastal patrols. His sister might not be any kind of sea dog yet she put him to shame with her high spirits and calmness as the sturdy *Rafaela* sailed deeper and deeper into the danger zones.

'The wind is exciting, is it not, Miguel?'

'Very exciting. I throb with the excitement.'

'How far now?'

'Too far.'

'Have courage, brother.'

Her laughter drifted back to him like music. Miguel was unmarried. Were he to wed it would be to a woman just like his sister. And if he could be as happy in wedded life as Evalina was in hers, he might even be prepared to give up the sea and take a boring job ashore in order to keep a jealous eye upon the lady.

'What are those lights, Miguel?'

'Either a giant freighter bearing down upon us or the coast authorities coming out to arrest us.' The captain of the *Rafaela* simply refused to be anything but pessimistic tonight.

The lighted vessel passed by on the starboard side. Just another old scow battling the midnight weather of the Gulf. Evalina's slender hands were strong on the wheel as they continued to nose through the heaving swell. Her brother appeared at her side, the smell of his pipe drowning out the multiplicity of sea scents billowing upwards from the deeps.

'It is not too late for me to put you ashore, sister.'

She didn't laugh now.

'We shall see it through together,' she stated, dark hair billowing. 'As we agreed.'

'As you agreed. You husband will cut out my heart when he finds out that I allowed you to force me to bring you north with me.'

'My husband will be in your debt for ever,' contradicted Evalina, rubbing her swelling abdomen. 'All of us will, my husband-lover, myself, little Christina here, and of course our sweet brother Lino most of all.'

Uplifting sentiments. Yet Miguel the brave sea captain was not reassured as he took the wheel again. The last of his family to travel this far north was Uncle Guillo. He'd marched with Santa Ana. Unlike Miguel, Uncle Guillo had no option but to keep travelling north until getting the living shit blown out of him at San Jacinto by Sam Houston. There was nothing to stop him swinging the *Rafaela* about and running for home except his sister. Petite Evalina who had tamed and then wed one of the most formidable men in all Mexico, would surely make mince out of Miguel were he to show the slightest sign of faltering now. And if she didn't kill him, brother-in-law Max certainly would. By comparison, Uncle Guillo had likely had it easy up here.

★　★　★

'What are you doing, kid?'

Jody started. He had not heard Udo come up behind. Moving about silently was one of the gunman's habits which he regarded as a talent. He also believed himself to be a snappy dresser, which explained today's black shirt, white bandanna and the cuffs of striped calico pants thrust into hand-tooled boots of Spanish leather.

And, of course, the guns.

Staring up at the man from where he sat on the lower stoop-step, the boy's stare focused on the sixshooter handles thrusting aggressively out of cutaway holsters. All kinds came through a trail station but Jody Wheeler had never encountered anyone quite like this man from the South before.

He hated him, hated them all. Had done ever since he found that bag of guns in the loft. Or had it been even before that?

Adults often commented on Jody's wisdom and perception, unusual in someone his age. At times the boy felt he could see right through people, see their lies and duplicity. He had never been close to his father for that reason, and in a reverse way, saw his mother as a saint.

Telly Udo he saw as akin to the Devil.

'Go away,' he pouted.

Udo nudged the boy's back with his

knee. Naturally he was grinning, wheezy suppressed laughter hissing through locked teeth.

'Why don't you like me, kid? I see you running after Mitchell like a little lapdog. How come you give me the cold shoulder?'

'You made Cord go away.'

'Hey, you are right on the money there. Yessir, sent old soberbones Cord packing, so I did. But just as well, heh? He had your mom in tears last night. Did you know that about old soberbones Cord?'

Jody looked away. For all his precocity there were many things he did not understand. Cord's overnight disappearance, for instance. His mother's tears. Neither did he understand why these men were still here at the time of year he liked best, when he and Joachim could go clamming, or his mother would take him into Bell's for a treat.

The dog came running up and Jody put his arms about its neck. 'Get him, boy. Go on, chase him off.'

'Ah, if it was only that easy,' Udo chuckled, leaping nimbly down on to the hard-packed earth of the yard to land lightly as a butterfly with sore feet. 'But you should know, kid, that fellers like me don't get chased, we chase. Like I chased your mom's boyfriend off last night. And you just never know who else might show up here that I might have to see off.'

He tapped the side of his nose and winked.

'Matter of fact I've got a real strong hunch that you are going to have more winter folks stop over real soon, folks that I might have to, you know, deal with.'

Without a word of warning Udo cleared both pistols in a flashing two-hand draw, causing the child to blanch with sudden terror.

Udo's laughter burst. 'Hey, look at the tough kid. Want mommy to change your pants, sonny? Look, a word of advice. When things start to pop hereabouts, and they surely will, get mommy to wrap you in cotton wool and hide you under her bed, otherwise . . . '

His words trailed away. Connie had appeared at the far end of the porch in apron and hair-curlers.

'What are you doing, Mr Udo?' she demanded, hurrying forward. 'Are you scaring him? Put those guns away.'

Udo's left cheek ticced as he stepped back a pace. The .45s blurred on his trigger fingers in whirring blue arcs. He flipped them, caught them, slid them into leather and folded his arms in a blurring sequence of supple actions that the eye could not fully follow. His eyes were ice-chips as Connie drew Jody to his feet and held him against her legs. 'Mother and child,' he sneered. 'The Virgin Mary and little Jesus.'

'Don't blaspheme,' he was told. 'I'll not have that here. And if it comes to that, I don't think I want you here any longer, Mr Udo, you or your friends.'

'Ahh, what a difference between what we want and what we get. But to set your mind at rest, lady, we'll be leaving you sooner than you think. See? Knew that'd cheer you.'

'When?' Jody asked quickly.

'Well, there's the catch, I'll allow.' Udo was enjoying this, his cheek-creasing grin genuine now. 'The when of it.' He gazed up at the moving skies. 'Guess we'll be going when we have done what we came to do.'

He halted abruptly as Stein and Frick appeared around the north corner of the building.

'Hi, pardners,' he said, going to meet them. 'Just keeping the family entertained. They are all cut up about Mitchell quitting, would you believe? I'd say that was a good thing, wouldn't you agree, Max?'

His manner was mocking but it was plain Stein was not amused. He glared a warning at Udo, who only smirked, flipped his hat into the air then caught it between thumb and forefinger.

'Mitchell gone, who'll be next?' he

half sang. 'If only we knew, we wouldn't be so vexed.'

As the three moved off, little Jody had one of his perceptive moments. He saw clearly that Max Stein wanted to silence Udo, yet held back. He might have been afraid; Jody could not be sure about that. But when he glanced up at his mother he saw fear in her eyes as she stared across at Telly Udo, and that made him feel both afraid and mad at the one time. For of all their winter guests, each one of them seemingly made of harder stuff than any men the boy had known, Udo, from the first day, was the one who disturbed them most; himself, the yardman, Mary and Jinko, his mom and even Joachim, although certainly not Crow Woman whom you couldn't imagine ever being afraid of anybody. The only one who seemed to have Udo's measure was Cord, and now, incomprehensibly, he was gone, just when Jody sensed they might need him most.

The men were drifting away, and

glancing across at his mother, the boy sensed that, in that uneasy moment, she too was thinking of Cord. Again.

★ ★ ★

The prison coach was forced to climb as if it were part mountain goat when the trail from the rangeland into the coastal hills grew steeper. The prisoner rattled his chains and offered a droll comment on the discomfort which only drew a faint smile from Hanline and no reaction at all from Marshal Prade.

Lino Guardia sighed as he gazed out through the rifle port in the metal plate, taking in the trees, hills and distant blue ocean.

'What a poem one could make of all this great beauty if only there was time. So much that is lovely, so little time to enjoy it all.'

'My brother writes poetry,' Hanline responded — anything to relieve the tedium. 'He once wrote — '

'No consorting with the prisoner,

thank you, sir,' snapped Prade.

'Consorting?' Guardia queried with mock innocence. 'Surely the marshal is mistaken. Is not the consorting that which the *caballero* and his *señorita* do beneath the sheets in the darkness when her mother is out and he is feeling so horny he — '

'Silence!' Prade removed his hat and patted his thinning hair, more deeply than ever antipathetic towards such things as Mexico, Mexicans, escort chores, or travelling in a vehicle too heavy to be well sprung. What he did like was seeing justice, sweet justice, dished up to those who made a mockery of it. 'Save your wit and wisdom for the Kingsville judge, killer. Who knows? He might even invite you to make a speech before you are dragged out and hauled up a tree on the end of a rope by your scurvy, lying throat.'

'Texas will never execute Lino for such a small thing as robbing a bank, Señor Marshal. And this is where you make the great mistake in not returning me to the Mexican authorities when I was unluckily captured on your soil.' The fluent spread of manacled hands was pure Spanish. 'In San Bonito, for the thing they say I did at Los Santos prison, I would be hanged, drawn and quartered and fed to the jailhouse dogs, for sure and certain. So you see where your hatred has led you? You — how do they say it — defeat your own purpose. No?'

This contention was pure fantasy as the lawmen were well aware. The truth of the matter was that the *bandido*'s arrest was almost threatening to become an international incident, due largely to his excessive popularity back in his home province, where they called him Caballero, and where it was highly unlikely they would find any fault with him even if he were to sail across the high seas to Rome and shoot the Holy Father without even affording him the opportunity to confess his sins.

Guardia was indeed the romanticized

hero all over Catarina Province, and its seaport capital, San Bonito, but up here by stark contrast he was the detested, vainglorious, wetback *bandido* who'd made infamous his personal proclamation: 'I am the enemy of Uncle Sam and the hero of all my people.' The Lone Star was salivating to swing this desperado, and there was malicious relish in Prade's tone as he said: 'You are a dead man, outlaw. The graveyard stink has been coming off you ever since you were arrested. You'd be better occupied making your peace with your Maker than trying to con an old pro like me. Why don't you face up to the fact you're going to die, and deserve every inch of hemp you'll get? You'd feel a better man for it.'

'I am too young to die, Señor Marshal.'

'Should have thought of that before you robbed the Kingsville bank. And before you pulled that crazy stunt at Los Santos pen.' Prade snorted in disgust. 'Look me in the eye and tell me that wasn't the most damnfool thing any chilli-eating thief ever pulled.'

'Ahh!' Lino Guardia sighed tragically, leaning back and closing his eyes. 'What I did at Los Santos . . . '

He was slipping back nostalgically to a day when all Mexico was bathed in brilliant sunshine and even infamous Los Santos prison appeared almost welcoming on the inmates' once-a-year visiting day. It was a day when everything seemed to smell of sweet success to Lino 'Caballero' Guardia as he guided his strawberry roan down out of the brooding sierras and over the green hills for the prison, with the intention of staging the greatest jailbreak in the history of this benighted valley.

Languishing in dark Los Santos in that mid month of winter was his *compadre* and brother-in-law, an innocent man and victim-hostage of the infamous *Regulares* of Castillo Valley, against whom Guardia and his freewheeling band from neighboring peaceful

Catarina Province had long been fighting on behalf of the poor and oppressed 'shirtless ones' for some years now.

Totally innocent of any criminal activity since settling down to married life with the former Señorita Evalina Guardia, Max Stein had nonetheless been abducted and thrown into Los Santos by the *Regulares* in an attempt to goad him into hot-headed reaction and thereby bring himself destruction at their hands.

The *Regulares*' next move was to publicly demand from Guardia an impossibly massive ransom, if Lino and his precious sister ever wished to see Big Max alive and in one piece again.

Of such violent and convoluted affairs did Mexican life largely consist in regions where one province might have as its hero a wild but colorful brigand such as Caballero Guardia, who happened to be the fiercest thorn in the side of the corrupt, discredited and officially decommissioned former

Federale force which still dominated by brute force and terror the region it had once legitimately ruled, Castillo Valley.

This was criminal corruption masquerading as law enforcement — but of course this was Mexico.

There was but one possible way a proud rogue and rebel could respond to so naked a challenge from a hated enemy — and Lino loved his sister, his reputation and, yes, even his brother-in-law too deeply not to take it.

Despite the light-hearted manner he exhibited *en route* to his destination today, the *bandido* rode with the certain knowledge that this was the big one; make-or-break time for Lino Guardia and the mortal enemies of himself and all Catarina Province.

He had invested much time, planning and plenty of hard cash stolen from the *Americanos* in today's ambitious operation, yet Los Santos could still prove a tough nut to crack. But with a dozen disguised henchmen already within the prison walls, carrying forged documents establishing them as kin of various inmates, and with a cache of arms secreted in the mess hall, Caballero was fully primed to have himself a day of matchless excitement and high adventure which would write his name even larger in the annals of the province, and most tellingly of all, earn the undying gratitude of both his brother, and his sister Evalina, whom, in typically florid Spanish style, Lino and Miguel worshipped as the very ideal of womankind.

The prison loomed.

With black hair dyed red, false mustache, attired like a gender-challenging denizen of dim border bars and armed with brilliantly forged documents affirming his identity as some bloody-handed inmate's only offspring, Guardia was soon safely inside and ready for action — readier than he'd ever been in his on-the-edge life.

And might well have been soaking up the sunshine of San Cristobal as an object of lust and abandoned adoration by scores of moist, red-lipped and over-sexed young virgins whilst accepting the acclaim of his hero-worshipping home city following his daringly successful rescue of Big Max Stein this very day — but for the black hand of evil coincidence.

Which struck savagely when, having personally put three block guards out of action with a gunbutt, Lino personally oversaw the adroit smuggling out of a lavishly disguised Max Stein, and was rounding up his henchmen beneath the unsuspecting scowls of the pen's brutish guards in the Big Yard when a sudden familiar voice turned his hot Spanish blood to ice-water in his veins.

'Guardia, you old villain. Who's toggin' you out these days? Been a time, huh . . . you miserable son of a scumsuckin' whore!'

Before him, a gringo face from the past. His outlaw past in Texas. A bitter enemy. One with his big mouth wide open now bellowing his name at the top of his lungs to galvanize a dozen gunpacking overseers in *Regulare* blue tunics into hysterical action.

'Guardia?' they were screaming, eyes rolling in wild panic. 'Who? Which? Where?'

He was sprung.

But course they could not hold him.

Not Caballero.

He was half-way to the main gates while the men in blue were still clawing for their *pistolas*. Lino Guardia, survivor of countless Yankee ambushes, was a lightning bolt, a will-o'-the-wisp and a Mexican jumping bean all rolled into one when the chips were down.

Even so, the bunch still had to shoot its way to their horses once outside, a passage of arms that proved gory and gruesome even by Castillo Valley standards.

But true to his talent, luck and reputation, sole survivor Guardia himself added three more enemy dead to his tally before bounding into his saddle and storming away, waving his sombrero and shouting obscenities.

And that should have been that. But of course it wasn't.

Lino Guardia was the *Regulares*' Enemy *Numero Uno* in Castillo Valley and he'd just reversed their elaborately contrived scheme to snare him with flamboyant and brutal success.

Max Stein freed, Guardia on the run, dead and wounded piled high around the prison's main gates.

What else could any raging *Regulare* still fit to sit a saddle do but take off after him, then run him like a honey bear chased by a relay of hounds? Harrying him remorselessly eighty miles northwards across cattle range, woodland and bleak reaches of desert until the exhausted fugitive plunged gratefully into the Rio Grande, to promptly tumble like a treasure beyond price into the welcoming arms of Rangers who hated him even worse than did the howling, weeping *Regulare* possemen he left behind him on the southern shore.

Ahhh, the memories!

Jolting along in the gray prison van with his eyes still closed, Guardia could not help but grimace as the images of what might have been his finest hour turned sour as swill.

But only for Caballero.

Due to the way things had panned out, with the *Regulares* focusing all their wrath and manpower upon his brother-in-law, Max and his escorts had made an unimpeded getaway, crossing the ranges to reach Catarina free and unscathed. This meant Operation Max had been a huge success, Lino reflected. It was just too bad he would have to die for it now.

But surely this was unworthy of the hero of San Bonito, to be thinking that way? he asked himself critically. Undoubtedly, was his personal response. For the great venture had succeeded even if its architect must now pay the supreme price. And opening his eyes to gaze out at the classic Texan landscape of brush and cows beneath an immense gray sky, he forced himself to conjure up a tender scene in San Cristobal that might be being enacted at that very moment, thanks to himself, brave Lino, who loved his family. A tall *Americano* was embracing the lovely young woman heavy with his child, tears of happiness streaming down her cheeks — and hopefully the name of Lino on everyone's lips.

His was a small price to pay and he loved them all, sister Evalina, brother Miguel and brother-in-law Max. 'Take care of her, *hombre*,' he murmured benevolently. 'And never leave my sister's side again.' He had never felt nobler as jolting wheels carried him onwards for the coast where the judges and hangmen waited. 'She and the little one to come are now in your hands, Big Max. Lino can never help you again.'

He dabbed at his eyes. Life could never get too dramatic for the Caballero.

7

Hardcase Hotel

The cornfed chippy with the frizzed red hair and wide brown eyes was pretty as a painting and scarcely more animated. Built on stirring lines and showing lots of bare flesh as she lolled against the bar puffing a crooked black Mexican cigar, she was used to having her tricks do all the hard work both here at the bar and upstairs in the bedroom.

Yet the most interesting male to cross her gunsights in a long time was proving disappointingly detached and remote, so much so that she was eventually driven to stir herself into a more active role.

'How about it?' she said. Not subtle, but honest.

'What?'

'You and me. The beast with two backs. Buck naked and smothered in whipped cream.' She was starting to get herself whipped up now, never mind the dairy products. She leaned closer and ran a finger along the inside of his thigh and licked beestung lips. 'Ever considered just how much body heat two people can cook up on a cold and rainy day, Mr Mitchum?'

'Mitchell.'

'Whatever. So?'

'So — what?'

'How about it?'

Cord was not concentrating. He was here to get drunk, not laid. He focused on the face before him as though seeing it for the first time, and was offended.

'Don't take this personal, lady, but get lost.'

'Told you he ain't your type, Helga,' advised the barkeep. He winked and chuckled. 'Not desperate enough, I reckon.' For a lethargic piece of trade, Helga could move fast when aggravated. Her reticule caught the man across the chops and he was seeing stars. On her feet, she hauled her arm back as though to give Mitchell the same treatment, but something stopped her, most likely the deadly flat stare he gave her over the rim of his glass. In this largely boozed-up barroom, Helga was cold sober and clearly caught the whiff of danger.

'Who needs you?' she said loudly, storming off. Then, 'Is there such a thing as one man who ain't limp-wristed or drunk in this so-called man's town, damnit?'

The eyes of customer and barkeep met in silent understanding. The latter poured another redeye and money changed hands.

'My last,' Cord announced to nobody in particular, and toted the glass off to a corner table where he would not be bothered further.

This shot would be his last, not because he'd had enough but because the liquor was failing to do what he was asking of it.

He drank and scowled at his glass. Tasted like swamp water and just about as effective. He'd had more success knocking the hard stuff back out at the hotel insofar as it had enabled him to take the first of two steps. Step one had been to find the guts to tell the truth. Step two was to stop looking for excuses and, having now quit the hotel, quit the goddamn county and put *finito* to the whole damn thing.

Head west for the open range, maybe. Trim the suckers in Laredo. Drink it down like a genuine hard-nosed high-roller, which was likely all he really was anyway even though he'd just lived through a couple of really good weeks thinking that maybe he might make it as something else.

And heard again her calling his name as he staggered from the hotel, sounding almost as though she was not angry, even as if she somehow understood or had expected to hear the terrible admission he had just made.

Or was he just imagining this to

make himself feel a little better? Have another, Mitchell. OK, Mitchell, one for the road.

'You look like hell, Mr Mitchell.'

This was not Mitchell speaking to Mitchell. This was the gruff voice of Bell's Landing law.

The sheriff was a stocky little man of forty, dark-skinned, a drum of a belly, bowed legs. He'd arrived at the saloon some time earlier to break up a brawl. Mitchell gave him the fish eye. The whole world was hostile tonight. He didn't want any lousy company in this lousy dump, even if he liked the lawman well enough.

'Get lost, Sheriff, this is a private wake.'

'Who died?'

'Mitchell the dumb dreamer. You're talking to Mitchell the card sharp now.'

'That odd bunch still out at the hotel?'

'I wouldn't know.'

The sheriff's eyes narrowed. 'You and Mrs Wheeler, Mitchell. Have you been discussing Corpus Christi by any chance?'

The tinstar already knew the truth of Wheeler's death. The Corpus Christi marshal's official report on the incident had accompanied the casket to Bell's. Mitchell had insisted he should carry the burden of informing the widow, and the sheriff had agreed. Well, he'd done his duty and look where it had gotten him. The last thing he wanted now was to talk about it.

'Mitchell, I — '

'Get lost.'

'You're drunk, man.' The sheriff seemed surprised. 'You sure there's nothing you want to tell me?'

Mitchell shook his head but the badgeman stood his ground.

'You confessed, didn't you?'

Cord stared. 'What?'

'Our secret. The part you played in Wheeler's death. You said you'd level with Miz Connie, and the way you're drinking, I guess you've done it.' A pause. 'I bet a buck she took it OK.'

Mitchell was offended by the man's seeming flippancy. He stiffened and made to rise from his stool, but a hand on his shoulder stopped him.

'Relax, man. I'm not guessing, you see. I know. Miz Connie came to me yesterday to ask for the truth. Claimed Crow Woman told her you killed Thad, and what did I know about it? Put on the spot like that, I had to 'fess up. Then I showed her the marshal's report from Corpus Christi, and she didn't turn a hair or shed a tear. Said she just felt sorry for you carrying this weight around without feeling you could tell her. So if you're worrying about forgiveness, gambler, you're forgiven.'

Mitchell sat dazed for several minutes, shaking his head in disbelief, yet knowing it was true. She had not reacted when he confessed, because she already knew. She knew — yet had treated him just like always. Goddamnit, he almost hated her for being so kind and understanding, for somehow this seemed to be undermining his decision to leave.

'It . . . it just doesn't figure,' he said wonderingly.

'Does to me, mister. Thad Wheeler was a bastard through and through as everyone knew. Connie and her kid are far better off without him . . . and, hey, you're not having another, are you?'

He sure was. And as the lawman moved off in disgust, he realized he was getting a little fuzzy at last. He began to relax. It was still broad daylight. Still plenty of time yet to fork and ride, he assured himself, frowning with faint interest as he turned to see what this latest ruckus was about.

There was always a fight going on somewhere in the sprawling, draughty, barnlike structure that was Cameron's Bar, which stood just off the main stem at the dock end of Bell's Landing.

This applied especially to Saturdays when the riders came in off the spreads and the fishermen left their boats bobbing at the jetties and engaged in free and open competition to see who could drink most, spend fastest and aspire to become bare-knuckle champion of Storm Bay, if only for this one weekend.

The women flocked to the bars with their men. Alongside Cameron's was a low-roofed manger where the women left their babies and children in the care of a massive and impassive Indian woman with yellow eyes. There they were fed, slept, cried or played while their parents set out to drink down sun and moon next door.

Here, there was always a pretty girl with up to four or five contenders for her favors, which could be as sure to strike sparks as an unshod brake on a locomotive. There was, at any given time, always at least one female screaming, or laughing hysterically, or falling to the floor. It was traditional. And of course there were always the men, crowding, jostling, competing, shouting, boasting, weaving their way through the thick blue smoke ready for anything and everything the bar could provide, especially violence.

This time it was a wide-bodied plant hand versus two tough deputies who made extra money keeping the peace here on their days off.

But Cord's interest quickly waned and he found his eye instead drawn to a plain-looking couple seated close together on a wall bench holding hands and sipping soda from the same bottle.

And it started an ache in him which saw him thrust the glass away and rise to his feet, knowing at last he could leave, that he must. When you began envying some loser in a patched shirt just because he had someone who thought enough of him to share the same soda bottle, he figured a man had had more than enough.

Bell's Landing paid little attention to the tall horseman in the slicker riding off through the rain some time later; he paid no attention to the town beside the restless bay.

As he reached the south trail he looked south-east to see the familiar looming shape of Devil's Spur dimly visible through the thinning curtain of rain.

He was glad when trees cut visibility down to just a few yards. He was packing a flask of redeye but doubted he would drink it now. The pressure that had stemmed from the decision to make a clean and honest break, despite what the lawman had told him, was receding now. It was still best he ride on. There was still nothing for him here; not for a man like him, so he advised himself, straightening his back and squaring his jaw. And thought: maybe instead of Laredo he would keep on south all the way to Mexico this time. Never been there before. Better climate and legendary card games. Big spotted cats prowling the trail-sides and *Rurale* lawmen every bit as dangerous as the *bandidos* they chased through the sierras. Sounded attractive to a wandering man who might not be quite as sober as he thought.

It was late afternoon and a ship's bell

sounded faintly across the bay as the horse broke into a trot and the rain began to ease.

Then he was atop a slight rise in the road looking down on the fork where the stages swung off the Gilmour Trail to make the half-mile run to the hotel and trail station.

There was a sign down there which read: TO THIEF CREEK HOTEL. He could not see the sign at that moment for the reason that it was obscured by the coach-and-four coming up from the south, and turning in right in front of it, headed on down the Thief Creek road.

Mitchell reined in sharply.

The coach was a dull and rain-streaked gray and resembled a dreadnought with its armour-plated flanks and rifle-port window slits. A driver in weather gear and a husky guard toting a big shotgun occupied the shielded high seat. Two unsaddled horses were tied to the rear gunnel rail, damp hides steaming as they followed the prison van off the trail down the loop road.

That it was a prison van there was no doubt, any more than there was any doubt it was making for the hotel.

Cord sat his motionless horse for long minutes after the equipage had been swallowed by the woods. Casting his mind back, he recalled Connie mentioning another party of guests scheduled to arrive today. She had not defined the make-up of that booking, perhaps was not aware that it would comprise armed guards and quite possibly lawmen and prisoners. They didn't haul those big rigs about just for the exercise, he knew. Most often when you sighted one there was some slavering wife-killer or bloody-handed outlaw chained inside.

Headed for Connie's place in this late afternoon. Where she was already playing hostess to a bunch of guests who just might be hardcases themselves.

Five shady or at least semi-shady house guests now augmented by

— what? Hardnosed lawmen escorting one or more criminals? The hotel was doing business, but what sort of trade was this for God's sake?

The horse was growing restive. He gave the animal its head and followed the trail down to the turn-off where the prison van's heavy wheel tracks cut deep in the mud.

Here he halted again. The horse pranced. He cuffed its ear and it stopped.

He still felt he should ride on. How could he face her again now, or the boy for that matter?

But what if she needed him?

And what about little Jody, for that matter. Hadn't that kid had enough heaped on to him in the past weeks without finding himself confronted with possibly even more trouble?

Of course he had no cogent reason for assuming the arrival of lawmen and prisoners automatically suggested trouble, he reasoned. Then in his mind's eye he conjured up images of

hulking Frick, giggling Udo and Big
Max Smith and their cache of weapons,
and it suddenly seemed easy enough to
sniff the wind and detect in it more
than just woodsmoke, rain and salt air.

He heeled the horse abruptly and it
jumped forward, startled. But they were
no longer travelling the main trail;
instead, they followed the loop road
down. He was just going down to check
up, he assured himself. She must hate
him now even if she didn't show it,
hopefully might order him to hell and
gone on sight. But he would still take a
look to make sure they were both all
right. She and the kid. He didn't want
to, but couldn't help it. Surely that told
him something he almost certainly
didn't want to know.

*　*　*

Jody rubbed condensation from the
dining-room window and peered inside.
His eyes widened when he saw the
Mexican prisoner in manacles slouched

at a table with a gun guard standing directly behind his chair. The two marshals were talking to Joachim by the servery while the driver hungrily wolfed down cheese and crackers as an appetizer before supper.

Max and his friends occupied various tables, smoking and sipping their drinks and not appearing very interested in the late arrivals, who by contrast interested Jody greatly.

There was no sign of his mother. She did not share his excitement over their latest guests' arrival either. Told him she had been expecting them all along. That they had booked by wire from Harlingen out along the Rio in the cattle country. Had Jody known they were expecting a wild Mexican *bandido* he would have told the whole world.

The boy almost stumbled over the dog as he turned away to go running across the yard.

The strange armour-plated vehicle stood squat and solid in the lamplit barn. Jody circled it warily. It was like some hulking gray monster with the dark slits in the sides resembling eyes. He touched it and it was cold, he sniffed and detected oil, grease and body odor.

The dog whoofed and Jody swung at the sound of a footfall.

'Cord!'

* * *

Lino Guardia was chuckling again and the marshals just couldn't figure him. Here was a desperado of the worst stripe just a day away from a courtroom with its own gallows in back, plus judge, jury and a swag of damning evidence, all waiting just for him, yet all he could do as he sat back sipping his coffee, winking at the sober proprietress and the giggling maid, was make jokes.

Could it be that after all his years of danger, life on the run and always the shadow of the noose hanging over him, Prade mused, the notorious plunderer of Texas banks was resigned to his fate, perhaps even weary of his violent life.

Testy Prade shook his head at the thought. No. Not this one. Lino Guardia was relaxed and joking because he did not expect to die, yet how he could possibly think otherwise the marshal couldn't figure.

Then an unsettling thought struck. The prisoner had been in good spirits ever since leaving the border, he realized, yet he'd not been half as light-hearted *en route* as he had been ever since they reached their hotel here on Storm Bay. It was, though, the moment Guardia sighted staff and guests that the last vestige of any possible seriousness was gone, leaving him acting more like a lawman than a lawman's prisoner.

And not for the first time did Marshal Prade's sober eye flicker critically over the faces around the big room where all the guests were gathered — the tall and impressive fellow they called Big Max and his vacationing friends.

His lawman's nose crinkled. Maybe he was obsessive about his work, sniffing out crime and criminals in every corner, but surely at least one or two of this fishing party looked just like the breed a peace officer would naturally want to check out on sight under different circumstances.

'Ah, such kindness,' Guardia was saying as the Wheeler woman placed a pad beneath his manacled wrists in order that he might drink his coffee more comfortably.

'Tell me, *señora*, would it be possible for you and your gentle friends here to perhaps attend my big trial in the big gringo court? Lino has few friends north of the border, and some friendly faces in the crowd would perhaps help him find the courage to die like a real hero.'

He sounded so genuine and appealing that suddenly Prade found the staff and a couple of the other guests turning to look at him almost accusingly. His cheekbones flushed.

'Don't fall for this guff,' he said gruffly. 'Palaver and buffalo dust are part of this outlaw's stock in trade. Let me remind you of what happened in Mexico before the Rangers caught him. Mounted an attack on a penitentiary for some fool reason, so he did, and when it was all over there were several dead and twenty wounded. All thanks entirely to Señor Lino Guardia, as low a snake as ever walked, of this you can be sure.'

'The marshal's right folks,' weighed in young Hanline, leaning in a doorway. 'He's due for what's coming his way, so don't waste your sympathy.'

'They say these cruel things, *señora*,' lamented Guardia, 'but all they wish to do is hang me for robbing the banks. I ask you. For years the gringos come to Catarina to cheat and plunder and steal our women. In return, all I do in return is empty out their banks. It is the balance of nature, nothing more . . . '

The clock on the wall chimed the hour and Max Stein consulted his heavy gold fob-watch. From beneath heavy level brows he glanced in turn at Udo, Frick, Clyde and Jackson, nodding in approval at the behavior of the last three and cutting a warning look at Udo who was flipping a .45 shell in the air and catching it.

He wondered momentarily about Mitchell then shrugged the thought away.

Right now, Max Stein was feeling good. Not relaxed, by a long shot, but relatively at ease now that Lino's arrival, the vital element in his whole grand plan, had been accomplished.

His brother-in-law had arrived dead on time and his boys were primed and ready for action. He foresaw no serious hitches and if he could rely on the seamanship and courage of sea captain Miguel Guardia, which he knew he could, then some time after dark tonight the sturdy *Rafaela* would nose quietly into the bay by which time he expected to have freed Lino and be ready to disembark for the sunny south.

Big Max was nothing if not a superb organizer and, before going straight, had masterminded many a clever crooked deal on the owlhoot.

But nothing ever as intricate as this.

The day he learned Lino was in the hands of the Rangers, Max Stein had slipped straight into full action mode. His first move was to contact a spy at Harlingen who had been able, for a considerable sum, to provide him with the planned travel schedule of Guardia's armed escort. Instantly he identified the Thief Creek Hotel as his selected 'target area,' and within twenty-four hours, Miguel was sailing up the coast in his fishing boat and Big Max was across the Rio recruiting the talent he needed for Storm Bay at Diamondback.

Now all that remained was to free his brother-in-law from the custody of a pair of tough Texas marshals — easy when you said it quick.

This thought saw Max saunter off down the short passageway to the kitchen where Joachim stood behind a bench with an apron tied around his middle, impassively making preparations for the evening meal.

'And what's on the menu this evening, *compañero*?' he asked genially, producing a silver case to offer a slim cigar, which the man accepted. 'Duck, by the looks?'

Duck it was to be, cooked to Joachim's special recipe: Texas Wild Duck With Rice. Sounded good to Max Stein, fingering the pellets of dope in the pocket of his smart jacket which, one way or another, would find their way into the plates of Mr Prade and Mr Hanline later tonight, thereby hopefully averting the necessity of killing anybody in order to set Lino free.

Although Max Stein talked a tough fight, and had made his bones in the early days, he was now a genuinely reformed character. His Diamondback four were essential for the success of 'Mission Lino', but Big Max would only claim total success if next day's dawn saw them all safely on the high seas with Lino, heading south with nobody left over to be buried.

Returning to the main room with his cigar he was greeted by the sound of laughter as the prisoner indulged in a little more gallows humor.

Connie Wheeler stood in the outer doorway with the night forming a dark frame around her slender figure, calling to her son. The wind was rising and rustling the trees. Big Max fingered his mustache and listened to the sounds of the sea surging in the darkness. Could be more weather on the way.

8

First Blood

'It's the one called Udo that scares mom, Cord,' the boy said as they stood in the doorway of the barn. 'She pretends she isn't afraid but I know she is. He's always laughing and — '

'Sure, sure, Jody,' Mitchell cut in. 'But tell me more about this Mexican outlaw. What's he supposed to have done?'

Jody shrugged. 'I dunno. He's kinda funny though. I heard the marshals say they're going to hang him so I guess he must be real bad, huh?'

But Cord didn't answer, his eyes on the lights of the hotel as uneasiness nagged. He'd closed his mind to it before, but now he could be honest with himself and admit he'd been edgy about Max's bunch right from the outset. Which reminded him of something. He clicked his fingers and started off for the stables, Jody jogging at his heels.

'Where we going, Cord?' No reply. 'I'm sure glad you're back. Mom will be too. She cried and cried after you left. Why did you go like that, Cord? Don't you like it here with us anymore?'

Miracles could happen, he thought hopefully. If Connie really did understand, and could seemingly forgive, like the sheriff claimed, then maybe Jody could too. That was if he ever had to know, of course.

He led the way directly for the cache of revolvers and high-powered rifles the boy had discovered in the hay, but they were gone. Mitchell reached up and massaged the back of his neck and seemed to sense something in the windy darkness of this suddenly uneasy night, like electricity running ahead of a storm. Now he fully understood why he'd turned back earlier when he'd had the open trail and all of wide-open Texas before him. His instincts had been fighting with his self-pity and all the liquor he was drinking to warn him that everything was wrong out here. And with the disappearance of the guns came a cold feeling of urgency. He'd wasted enough time out here, and there was danger at the hotel. He could smell it. It was time to face it.

As man and boy hurried across the blustery coachyard, the meal hour was fast approaching. The places were all laid and Mary was showing guests to their chairs while Max Stein was in the galley insisting on giving a grumpy Joachim a hand with the food, which he neither needed nor appreciated.

Connie heard the footsteps on the gallery and went hurrying to the doors. 'Jody, is that you — ?' She stopped with her hand to her breast as the kid came in with Mitchell's tall, wind-blown figure filling the doorway behind him. 'Oh . . . oh, Cord, I'm so pleased,' she flustered. 'Er, Jody, go wash your hands.'

She squeezed Mitchell's arm and dropped her voice to a whisper.

'It's all right, Cord. The lawmen explained everything. We know Thaddeus tried to kill you . . . just as he's tried to kill others. We understand.'

He stared down at her, wanting to take her into his arms. Before he could act on that she put on her bright face and actually took him by the hand as though to prove what she'd just said. 'Now, come along, I'd like you to meet our new guests.'

He hooked his hat on the coat-rack and swept the room at a glance.

A barrage of stony glances was directed his way from the second table, where Max's party sat, as he acknowledged his introduction to Marshals Prade and Hanline first and one Lino Guardia second.

Reassured to see that everything seemed regular enough for the moment, Cord took a long second look at the notorious outlaw, who nodded amiably, black eyes twinkling.

'Señor Mitchell, please join us,' Lino Guardia invited cheerfully. 'But perhaps you should not sit too close to me with that big gun on your hip, or the good lawmen may get nervous, no, Marshal?'

But Mitchell remained standing as Big Max entered from the kitchen toting two plates of steaming Duck à la Joachim. 'Looks like some rain coming . . . ' he remarked but broke off when he realized Telly Udo was on his feet and advancing towards him.

'It's all right, Telly,' Max said sharply but the pale-faced hardcase shook his head.

'No it ain't, Big Max,' Udo disagreed, raking Cord up and down. 'Anything but all right, seems to me.' He halted. 'You leave, you come back, Mitchell. What's the game?'

Again Max interjected, but Udo made a side-ways chopping gesture with his right hand.

'You might be mostly right, but not

always, Max,' he hissed. 'Something stinks to high heaven here. He was snooping and acting nosy before, and you said yourself you were plenty relieved when he left. Now he's back, and I want to know whyfor — all things considered, that is.'

'Mr Udo,' Connie put in sternly, 'would you please sit down and let us get on with our m — '

'Shut your stupid mouth, sister.' Udo was building up to something here. 'Or I'll have to shut it for you.'

'Don't you talk to my mother that way!'

'You too, squirt. Everyone sit down and hush up while the drifter says his piece. OK, you got the floor, big man.'

Cord's lips were tight. 'Better show some respect, runt. You are speaking to a lady.'

'Runt? Why you long piece of shit — ' That was as far as Udo got as he lunged at Mitchell. He ran into a short right that cracked against his jaw and sent him tumbling to the floor, bloody-mouthed, as Big Max came rushing in.

'Damnit, Mitchell, what do you think you're doing?' he shouted angrily. 'Telly, are you OK?'

'The hell I am!' Udo mouthed, springing to his feet with a gun in his hand that none had seen him draw. He waved the barrel, shivering with emotion. 'Step aside, Max. This one's had it coming from the jump and by God he's gonna get it. Move, I say, damnit!'

With everyone in the room on their feet by now, the atmosphere was charged highly enough to lift the roof as a stunned Max Stein saw his entire operation threatening to disintegrate before his very eyes. But this was a capable man in a crisis. He recovered in an instant and went into action.

'You asked for it, Mitchell,' he panted, tugging Cord's .45 from its holster. Then he jerked a thumb to his men. 'Get him out of here and see he doesn't come back. Come on, you too, Udo, move your ass. All of you!'

He stepped back a pace to give the quartet room as they seized hold of Mitchell and hustled him through the front doors despite Connie's protests. As the doors banged shut on their backs, Max tossed the Colt carelessly on to the table and managed a reassuring smile.

'Sorry, everyone, Mrs Wheeler, Marshals. But we can't have that sort of behaviour, now can we? Please, sit down and let's continue with our meal. Everyone must be starving.'

It seemed not. An angry Marshal Prade hauled Guardia to his feet and shoved him towards the side door, free hand resting on maplewood gun handle.

'This is totally unacceptable, madam,' he bristled. 'I would certainly be intervening in this violence but for the responsibility of this vermin. I'm advising you that for security reasons we're shifting to the north wing which will henceforth be off limits to all, a curfew any man will ignore at risk of his life. Well, Marshal, get that fool door, man!'

Hanline jumped to obey and the three disappeared in an instant. Yet Connie didn't seem to notice or hear what was said. She was attempting to reach the main doors but Max blocked her off, raising a warning hand, palm forward. His face was stone-hard now. The incident had expanded into a major hitch in his plans and Stein was very angry.

'Please, Mrs Wheeler, don't force me to play rough. Just do as I say and everything will be fine. How about coffee all round?'

* * *

Cord hit the ground for the third time. Or was it the fourth? He was losing count as kicks and blows continued to rain down. Rolling on to one shoulder, all he could dimly see was a forest of legs about him. Vaguely he identified Udo's flashy, high-heeled boots. He

177

swung a high overarm punch, iron hard fist making brutal contact with spongy groin. There was a scream of agony and Udo was buckled over and spewing up his guts as Cord powered desperately to his feet, only to be sickened by a blow to the back of the head with a heavy rifle butt.

The night pitched and yawed in his vision and he knew he was badly hurt, maybe even concussed. Yet he still fought against going down again, sensing if he did he might never get up. Reeling and groaning as they attacked from all sides, he thought he was a goner when suddenly he heard other voices; sounded vaguely like Joachim first then maybe Big Max.

Then it was definitely Joachim's distinctively accented French-Indian voice that roared: 'He's had enough, damn you. I'll take care of him and guarantee he won't trouble you no more. Otherwise it's you boys against my double-barrel greener . . . and some days I just can't miss.'

Mitchell knew he would have fallen but for the powerful arm about his middle now. He thought he might have heard Big Max bark: 'If we see either of you again tonight you are dead meat, swamp man!' Then a vast black pool appeared at his feet and he was sinking into it.

* * *

The light was a pinpoint at first, a spot of silver in a black universe, which began to grow larger as he groaned and pain bit into him in a dozen places until finally concentrating in the back of his skull. The sliver of light continued to expand and grow brighter until it seemed to shiver and assume the shape of a giant flat spearhead.

No, he realized as pain threatened to lift off the top of his head and his eyes snapped wide. Not a spearhead. The blade of a huge skinning knife held close to his eye.

Then he remembered. He made a

wild pawing motion and the knife receded to be replaced by something almost equally fearsome. Crow Woman at six-inch range was an intimidating sight.

'He sees the light and the eyes are straight,' she pronounced, seeming to come from a great distance. 'So the brain is undamaged. All that is needed now is the potion.' Her huge knife slipped into the sheath hanging from her belt with a soft hiss of sinister sound.

Then she stepped back, her place taken by her husband.

'You sure got that little reptile a good one in the gonads, eh, Cord. Want a jolt before the potion? I can tell you you'll need it.'

'Yeah . . . no!' he corrected. No liquor. Not even now. A powerful arm slipped beneath his shoulders and hauled him into a seated position. The world shuddered on its axis and he knew his skull was splitting in two. But when he could see straight again he realized two things. He was in the boathouse and he was going to live.

Crow Woman's special Comanche potion would stop a charging bull buffalo in its tracks. But he had to have faith in any woman who could figure out what a man was thinking even before he thought it. Even so he coughed violently and protested feebly as the lizard-and-sulphur-tasting medication clawed its way down into his vitals. Somehow he straightened, eyes watering, and made a weak waving motion at Joachim who knew exactly what he wanted.

By the time he was half-way through his cigarette they'd strapped up his head and he was coming out of it. Not strong yet, but recovering fast. And mad. He wanted to go looking for people with a Colt .45 but knew he wouldn't. Not until he understood what the hell was going on, leastwise.

As though reading his thoughts, Joachim speculated soberly to his lady: 'It's got to have somethin' to do with that Mexican, Guardia. Has to. They came out in their true colors just now, but I saw them eyeing off the marshals and whisperin' among themselves well before Udo went loco. And now you sayin' you smelt owlhoot on 'em from the start, right?'

Owl Woman nodded and studied Mitchell with flat black eyes. 'Evil men exude an evil smell. Are you ready to fight?'

He blinked. Then nodded. Feeling readier by the minute, for the woman and boy were on his mind now. But he felt he should be able to walk properly before he went looking for more trouble. 'Give me five minutes.'

'You may not have that long.' Owl Woman took up a brightly painted gourd, shook it vigorously then sat with it clamped to her ear listening to the fading rattle. Her pet bat, hanging upside down from her interior washline, cheeped once and was still. She seemed to find this highly significant. 'Very little time,' she affirmed, gazing now at a shimmering sun-god medallion suspended from the rafters. 'The tide comes in, the wind rises and there is great danger for those you love . . . ' she intoned. Then she shrugged off-handedly, 'But of course if you wish to sit here smoking tobacco until Hallowe'en . . . '

Minutes later the three quit the floating home to make their way along the sandy beach towards Devil's Spur. Mitchell shook his head to clear it. Owl Woman had a way of getting you up and going, only trouble was his feet kept getting tangled and he occasionally saw double. But with the rough wind buffeting him and Joachim setting a solid pace, it wasn't long before he found himself able to straighten up and square his shoulders. He tugged at the sling holding Joachim's rifle over his shoulder then touched the butt of the .45 for reassurance.

His jaw set stone-hard as he lifted his head to look at the mighty bulk of the spur faintly outlined by stormy skies. And knew deep down he was ready to fight as never before and fill as many graves as needs be if that was what it took to ensure the safety of Connie, the boy and the others. No point in speculating on what they might find at the hotel, and as far as the mystery of Big Max and his bunch of hellers was concerned, they might well find themselves forced to shoot first and investigate later. With legs pumping, lean arms swinging now, the gambler knew he was readying to sit in on the highest-stake game of his career.

Joachim slowed to allow him to catch up. The big man was breathing heavily, pigtail twitching in the rainy wind.

'You OK now?'

'Never better.'

'How do you want to handle this, Cord?'

'Aren't you in charge?'

'After the way you ripped into those pecker-heads? No siree. You've earned the right to call the shots.'

'Right. The most important thing is our folks' safety. We'll come in quiet round the south wing and infiltrate to find out what's going on. If we find anyone's in danger, we'll start picking the bunch off one at a time from the dark. And if we have to start shooting, we'll do it fast and we won't miss.'

'Great minds think alike — hey, hold up. What's that?'

'Boat,' Crow Woman stated flatly as Cord turned to see a bobbing light in the dark bay waters. 'Comes from the ocean.'

'It's heading into the the jetty,' Cord said, pointing. 'Can you make it out?' he asked the man.

'Ridin' low in the water like . . . like one of them fat Mex fishing boats that wander up the coast from time to time. They never pull in here though. It's illegal. They gotta go in with a pilot further north.'

'Are you thinking what I'm thinking?' Mitchell asked after a long moment.

'That something this unusual might just be tied in with the something plumb unusual we got at the hotel?'

Joachim nodded briskly. 'I'm with you. But wait a minute. What do you make of this, sweetheart?'

'Trouble,' came Crow Woman's unhesitating reply.

The couple watched him expectantly. This was his decision to make, their silence told him. He still wanted to reach the hotel about five minutes ago, worry about mystery ships later. Yet the sudden appearance of the boat, now nudging in on the swell with figures dimly visible on the deck, was triggering off alarm signals in all directions.

A Mex boat plus a Mex outlaw plus Mex-loving Big Max and his bunch of bastards added up to — what?

Mitchell shook his head. The hell with the damned boat! His priorities lay at the hotel.

'Let's go,' he grunted, and was off at a long-legged lope before the wind had snatched his words away. Footsteps followed unhesitatingly. These were good people.

Pounding the warped and weathered

planks, he shot a glance back at the sound of the boat clunking up against the pylons and imagined he caught a shivering sheen of light on something slender and metallic; a rifle barrel maybe.

He slammed to a sudden halt, Joachim and Crow Woman almost piling into him. The man began to curse.

'Hush, damnit!' Mitchell panted, light sheening taut features as he raised his head to listen.

Footsteps.

Heading their way from the hotel just beyond the brush-grown bend in the jetty. His signal was instantaneous and unmistakable. All three leapt from the planking together to sprawl motionless in the deep surrounding gloom as a tall figure came lurching into sight, his head and wide shoulders framed against the mist-blurred lights of Thief Creek.

No risk of Big Max sighting them, he realized. He was rushing for the dock as eagerly and blindly as if it were

Christmas Eve and he'd just heard Santa's sleigh bells.

Ten would get you a hundred that the boat's arrival came as no surprise to Big Max.

9

Violent Night

A pale face peered down from a darkened second-floor window of the creaking north wing.

From that vantage point could be seen the rain-swept wagon yard lighted by a pair of hooded storm torches and enclosed on three sides by the wing with the north wall of the hotel to its left and the rain-streaming façade of the wagon shed and stables on the right.

Towards the bay-windowed west corner of the hotel heavy wooden storm doors covered the cellar entrance where sodden figures crouched behind cover, peering upwards across the weeping yard.

'That's the young one, Hanline, and he's a sitting duck, Max,' hissed Telly

Udo, his Colt cocked and ready in his fist. He tugged his hatbrim lower and cursed. 'Damnit! What are we waiting for? The lawdogs know we're after Guardia now, and they've told us to go straight to hell. Why hold back? We all know we're gonna have to go in after your greaser sooner or later, so what's wrong with right now?'

The gunslinger was eager, his henchmen less so. The violence triggered off by Cord Mitchell earlier had blown Stein's meticulously plotted plan of action through the roof. The intention had been to dope Guardia's escorts, set him free, then quietly slip him out of Texas aboard the expected *Rafaela* without even disturbing the night-roosting gulls down at the jetty.

Big Max had been proud of his plan. Still was, even though it was dead in the water. He needed another plan, and fast.

His henchmen waited with varying degrees of mounting impatience. The marshals were securely forted up in the wing with their prisoner, and now impatience, the weather and rye whiskey were working on Max Stein's party of four, less one. He'd assigned Jackson the chore of riding shotgun on the others inside ... and time was slipping by.

Why not make their big play now and do the job he'd hired them for, as Udo demanded?

Stein pondered, conscious of icy water trickling down his back. Hit them with all they had. But it wasn't that easy a decision for Max Stein, ex-outlaw with heavy emphasis on the ex. He didn't want gunplay to play any part in this operation and never had. He'd hired the Diamondback guns to guarantee his success, not as executioners.

And of course there was the most vital consideration of all in that Lino was in the hands of the enemy up there now, and there was no ironclad guarantee that those 'dedicated peace officers' might not put a bullet through his brother-in-law's skull if under attack rather than see such a 'desperado' go free.

He cursed suddenly as he checked out his fob-watch. It was twenty minutes past the scheduled arrival time of his temperamental brother-in-law Miguel and the *Rafaela*. And it was Big Max who'd stressed that split-second timing was essential to the success of the entire operation.

He didn't know the boat had arrived but would bet his life it had. And who was to say what Miguel would do if there was nobody on the jetty to greet him? Figure the operation had failed and set sail before the port authorities caught up with him? It could happen, and if it did then Operation Lino was dead in the water.

As usual, when a big decision must be made he made it fast.

'I've got to get to the jetty,' he announced, rising in a half-crouch. 'Just make sure nobody quits the wing, and keep your powder dry until I get back.'

The announcement invoked a storm

of protest, and big Frick slammed a hand against the storm covers, brute face lined faintly by yellow light spilling from the bay windows close by.

'The hell with that, Stein, that don't suit,' he almost snarled. Neither he nor Clyde were eager to tangle with the marshals, but like Udo, felt if the job was to be completed it had to be now. The enemy was at hand, the die was surely cast — and suddenly Max's procrastination was beginning to make him sound weak and indecisive.

Realizing he now had support, Udo confronted Big Max with a sneer riding his mouth.

'Let's face it, Max, you ain't been shaping up any too good since we got to this dump, have you? First you let Mitchell just wander off yesterday, even though a man with one eye could see he was playing some tricky game. Then when he gets back and raises hell, you don't let us finish the bastard like you know we should but let that damn Joachim cart him away like — '

'Mitchell's finished,' Max snapped. 'In any case — '

'And now,' Udo said as though he hadn't been interrupted, 'just when we've got this game by the throat again and are set to wrap it up, you want to run off to meet a boat.' He glanced round for support. 'Know what I think, Big Max? I think you've been living straight too long. Five years is a hell of a long time, especially when a man ain't as young and feisty as he used to be. You've gone soft, ain't that right, boys? We know how to save a job, and we're not scared to burn powder doing it. Ain't that right, boys?'

Two heads nodded and the tall man stiffened. This was insurrection. Max Stein squared his shoulders and spoke with the kind of natural authority that Telly Udo could never command, for all his deadliness. He was angry but still felt he owed them an explanation. His henchmen knew nothing about the *Rafaela* until now.

'Miguel's due at ten, and he will be

on time. The plan was for us to be waiting at the jetty with Lino ready to board when he showed, which would have been the case but for the delay. He'll be jittery as hell. If the coast patrol picks him up, with his record, he's a goner. If I don't get down there to reassure him he's just as likely to get the jitters and set sail for Mexico leaving us stranded, with or without Lino, goddamnit!'

'Some kind of greaser kinfolk you got if that's the best they can do, Max,' Udo sneered.

'Shut up, Telly.' Max confronted the killer squarely. 'We're doing this my way. I'll go reassure Miguel then get back here pronto and we'll free Lino no matter what the cost. That's the promise I made his family and San Bonito, so I can't break it. *Comprendes*? As for you taking over, mister — '

The lightning manner in which a .45 jumped into Big Max's hand and thrust against a startled Udo's flashy belt-buckle proved that the old days might well be gone but were anything but forgotten for one former rustler of the Rio Grande. In that tense moment, Big Max Stein looked bigger than ever.

Telly Udo's hissing, breathy giggle sounded as he backed up two paces, pale hands spread over gunbutts, face gleaming like a knife-blade in the rainy light. Stein cocked his piece with his thumb and Frick and Clyde moved aside when it seemed certain that the killer would go for iron despite staring death in the eye.

But typical of the man's mercurial nature, Udo's mad giggle suddenly died, he folded his arms and smiled amiably.

'Sure, whatever you say, Stein. You're picking up the tab after all. We'll follow orders. That's what we're here for, right?'

Max was only partially reassured by the surrender. But when a distant foghorn sounded from across the bay he knew there was no further time to waste. 'Damn right!' he said forcefully, and with a parting look of warning, turned and was gone.

Udo breathed. 'Sorry, Maxie, damn wrong was the right answer to that one.' He tugged one of his pale blue Turkish cigars from an inner pocket and stuck it between his prominent front teeth. 'Someone gimme a light while I tell you exactly how we're gonna pull old Max's irons out of this fire, boys. It's so simple it'd bring tears to your eyes.'

* * *

The two men hugged like brothers and pounded one another on the back as the thin sea rain continued to mist over the bobbing *Rafaela*, the jetty, and the tin-roofed shelter close by where Cord Mitchell crouched unseen and unsuspected.

'You made it, Miguel, you son of a gun!' Stein laughed, his face gleaming in the boat's dim lights. He clapped the fisherman's muscular arm. 'Knew I could depend on my brother-in-law to come through, *amigo* — '

'Speaking of brothers-in-law, *compadre*, where is Lino?' Miguel broke in. 'I do not see him with you.'

Max had his mouth open to reply when she appeared in back of Miguel like a lovely sea-goddess in black mantilla and and ankle-length cape which concealed her swelling beauty.

'Evalina!'

'Maximilian — my *chiquita*! Surprise, surprise!'

A grim-faced Mitchell dashed rain from his eyes as he watched Big Max leap aboard the craft to embrace the pregnant and improbably beautiful young Mexican woman in a huge bear hug. As the couple continued to kiss and hug — her appearance an obvious surprise for Max Stein — the bill-capped Miguel glanced anxiously in the direction of the half-hidden hotel, prompting Cord to do likewise.

'We could be running out of time, pard,' Joachim murmured at his side.

Cord nodded. For crouched there

with a fully loaded Colt .45 in his fist, he was almost astonished to realize in that moment just how ready he was — solid ready — to yet again risk his life and take any damn fool risk for someone other than single-minded Cord Mitchell himself.

It was a revelation to realize that maybe for the first time in his life others were more important than himself. That attitude, so new and unexpected, had first made itself felt in earnest the day he'd gone after the man who'd called himself Smith, not for selfish reasons of his own but simply because he'd sensed he represented some implied threat to the Thief Creek.

That feeling was far stronger right now as he realized that he didn't have to think twice about whether or not he was ready to to risk everything he had for Connie and her little boy. And saw it not as not some form of cheap heroism, but rather a privilege. And just had time to wonder if maybe all this signalled the welcome goodbye to the old selfish and single-minded Cord Mitchell, before Joachim gave him a reminding nudge.

'We're going aboard,' he announced without hesitation. 'If Max won't tell us what is going on, we'll make him.'

'Too bad my missus ain't here. She's real good at making folks do things they don't want to, her and that big cutter of hers.'

Only now did Cord realize Crow Woman wasn't with them. He glanced round but she had vanished. He shrugged, nodded to Joachim and then they were up and running. There was but one man aboard the *Rafaela* on full alert, and it wasn't Max Stein. The rugged Miguel emitted a shout of alarm as two large figures emerged through the gray rain, reached for a belaying pin, came up with it but ran straight into Mitchell's sweeping gun-barrel which dropped him senseless to the deck. At the same instant, Joachim's gun jabbed a whirling Big Max in the short ribs, and the startlingly beautiful woman gasped and clutched her swelling abdomen in alarm.

'Max!' she cried. 'Who are these *hombres*? And where is brother Lino?'

'That outlaw's your brother?' Cord demanded.

'Both are my brothers,' Evalina retorted, kneeling at the dazed Miguel's side. 'And Max is my husband, who will cut out your hearts and feed them to the fishes for what you do. Won't you, beloved?'

'All this sneaky son of a bitch will do if he doesn't start explaining every damn thing that's going on here,' Cord snarled, pressing his gunsights into the hollow beneath Stein's right ear, 'is die.' He pressed the gun harder. 'I mean it, pilgrim, start talking fast.'

Big Max had turned the colour of death as he swung his handsome head to stare past his captors at the distant, glinting roof of the Thief Creek Hotel, aware that he was helpless and with resistance or violence the furthest things from his mind right now. Although overjoyed that his wife had made the dangerous journey with her

201

brother, now, with two guns in his face and vital seconds clicking away, the mastermind and major domo behind the elaborate attempted rescue of Lino Guardia, which was now teetering on the edge of disaster, realized he had but one card to play: put his trust in Mitchell, a ploy he sensed might only pay off if he told the whole truth. And decisive as always, he proceeded to do just that. Fast.

'Listen,' he urged — and it all flowed out like a torrent. The tale of the *Regulares'* imprisonment of the reformed Max Stein — his real name — in the hope of snaring his wife's brother; Lino's recklessly successful attack upon Los Santos penitentiary to set his gringo brother-in-law free; Lino's flight and eventual capture by the Texas Rangers; Stein's pride and passion for his Mexican family leading him to plan, fund, organize and almost accomplish what would surely have been one of the most spectacular events in the history of South-west Texas's law annals, namely the Caballero's escape and safe return to Mexico, where he would again be safe in Catarina Province.

'They'll hang Lino if he goes to trial, Mitchell,' he concluded emotionally. 'Sure, he's a wild son of a bitch, but he's done more good for folks in Catarina than every crummy government they've got — '

'He is a saint,' Evalina cried passionately, and a recovering Miguel bobbed his head in full agreement. But they were doing little to assist Lino Guardia's cause with all this heavy-handed overstatement as far as Cord was concerned, and he was struggling to sift the wheat from the chaff in what he was hearing and seeing, when a woman's scream followed by a single shot sounded from the direction of the hotel.

Cord and Joachim stared at one another in horror. 'Miz Connie!' the latter shouted, and cleared the boat rail to hit the jetty running.

'I'm coming with you, Mitchell,' Max cried. 'If that means what I reckon it does, you're going to need me along to help handle my men.' He seized Cord by the arm as he made to break away. His expression was desperate. 'Nobody was to get hurt, you understand? Those were my orders, and you've got to believe me. I hired that bunch in case I needed them, but it was a mistake. You and I are on the same side, damnit. Give me my gun back and we'll see what we can save out of this.'

The gambler trusted few men, yet something desperate told him to take a huge risk and trust Big Max.

'Then let's go,' he almost snarled, thrusting the gun into Stein's hands and vaulting to the jerrybuilt jetty.

'All is lost,' groaned Miguel the dramatist as the running figures vanished into the sifting gray curtains of rain. 'I see now that from the very start, Max's great plan was doomed. They will all die, the port captains will seize the *Rafaela*, your bambino will be born behind prison walls and . . . '

His voice broke off. Sister Evalina was giving him one of her ferocious glares which were famous in their family, and her message was loud and all too clear.

'*Por favor*, forgive my cowardice, sister.' The captain buckled. 'Of course, we shall wait for them and fight alongside them, as you wish, and we shall then all sail home happily and safely to Mexico together.' Turning away for the wheelhouse he made the sign of the Cross on his chest and whispered, 'We are all dead. Oh, for a padre to cleanse Miguel of his sins before he meets his Maker!'

10

The Final Guns

Lino Guardia was sweating even though the north wing room was chill. With manacled hands in his lap and his desperate eye on the key dangling from the deputy's belt, he looked every inch a defeated man, yet in truth was far from it. His legs, roped to the medallion-back sofa supporting him, luckily lay in shadow. He was furtively working them furiously to and fro out of sight of his captors, and was finally almost convinced the thongs were at last beginning to stretch and weaken, when the slow-pacing Prade paused abruptly to glare suspiciously.

'Why the devil are you sweating, greaser?'

The man from the South was a

natural actor. He slumped. His eyes rolled white and fearful in their sockets. 'I . . . I think it must simply be because I do now finally fear the hangman. Señor Marshal sir. May the Virgin protect me.'

He thought that would do it, yet despite a flickering smirk of satisfaction at the prisoner's admission, the hawk-faced lawman was still drawing nearer for a closer inspection.

In desperation, Lino glanced out the window into the yard looking for something, anything, to divert the other's attention as he leaned towards him. The wind was rising and beating against the rattling panes. Across by the wagon shed to the right, a sudden gust caused the shrubs to twist in a frenzied fit of agitation.

Interesting but hardly a diversion. Then Lino's gaze cut in the opposite direction and instantly he stiffened on his sofa at what met his eyes. Suddenly there was no need to invent any diversion. It was already there, and his shock was totally genuine as he jerked forward in order to see better. '*Madre de Dios*! I knew Big Max chose the wrong *hombre* in that one. Look!'

Three faces stared down, and two gazed back up.

A picture of hardcase bravado, Telly Udo held his hostage before him like a shield, his gun muzzle touching Connie Wheeler's breast as the couple stood locked together in the open, in the wind and rain. Dim watching faces showed above the storm doors in back of Udo at the corner of the main building, where a bulging bay window blazed with light. The gunman's toothy smile defied the slanting rain as his voice rose in a shout.

'Waiting time's over, Marshals!' Despite the noise of the storm his words carried clearly to the upstairs windows where Marshal Prade and his deputy crouched low, clutching drawn guns. 'Her life and the snotnose's as trade for your prisoner. So get a shake on and make up your mind, on account of the wetter I get the itchier my finger gets, otherwise we'll finish 'em both and still take you.'

'Where is your boss?' Prade shouted back. 'If I deal with anyone it will be with him, you . . . you — '

'Winner, badgepacker, try winner!' Udo taunted, then spat a vicious curse as Connie suddenly attempted to break free. He snapped her head back, and with his left hand cupped beneath her chin, thrust her forward again. One short minute earlier she had been inside attending her child, the next found herself being dragged violently outside with a gun at her head, helpless and terrified.

Yet she had showed no outward fear then, refused to make another sound now, even with one gun at her breast and two more abruptly angling down at her from above as the marshals jerked open a window and trained sixguns on Udo's grinning head, so close to her own.

Instead she drew herself up straight

and tall, still taller than Udo, even when he raised himself on his toes to fill his lungs again. The man was fighting to stifle the crazy giggle as his emotions ran riot from the excitement.

'Countdown time, you sons of bitches! One . . . two . . . '

Having retreated prudently from the storm doors to the corner of the hotel under the bay windows when Udo made his big play, Clyde and Frick remained there, more as tense spectators than participants in the unfolding drama, too proud to cut and run yet too rat-cunning to back Udo's play by sticking too close and thereby placing their bodies on the line should the lawmen open up.

With their naked guns and hard faces, these badmen of Diamondback still managed to look dangerous, as indeed they were. Yet they appeared more like sitting ducks bathed in flooding lamplight to the eyes of the tall, rain-soaked figure who suddenly lunged into sight eighty feet away at the far corner of the hotel's ornate façade with a gun in his fist and two grim-faced men in back of him.

Mitchell hesitated momentarily to take in the scene. The long gallery was empty, the lighted windows casting squares of light upon wet boards. One deeply recessed door stood open, the other was closed. No sign of anyone within, but he heard a faint murmur of voices. He couldn't see what was taking place in the wagon yard which had Frick and Clyde so engrossed, but when he heard a wild shout he felt a tingle of alarm. Udo's crazy voice — he'd bet on it.

He shot one look over his shoulder at his companions. Joachim and Big Max, still panting from the hard run, stood rock solid and ready. They heard another wild shout above the rain, and that was all they needed to hear.

As one man they surged forward into a rushing run. Past the first windows of the octagonal-shaped front room where the fearful faces of staff and drivers stared out. On by the thickly arched doorframe of the front door with a glimpse of empty dark corridor and flocked wallpaper, then the alcoved landing where a teary-faced Jody Wheeler knelt up on a stool to see his hero rush by, tall and fierce-looking. Mitchell was within yards of the north corner and rushing at full stretch before big Frick sensed something and whirled, jaw sagging open and his revolver coming up as he saw the worst kind of trouble bearing down on them like an express train.

'Heads up!' he bellowed, and triggered, the snarling slug whipping between Mitchell's swinging left arm and his body to strike someone behind him.

Cord reached the man before he could trigger again. He hit like a pile-driver, turning one shoulder to use it as a weapon to smash the big hardcase off balance. His whipping elbow crunched into Frick's face and drove him back into a cursing Clyde, who was knocked off his feet by the impact.

The outlaws recovered with a speed born of desperation, and in the savage moments that followed, in a brutal close-quarters mêlée where a man couldn't shoot for fear of striking a friend, three desperate men with everything to fight for swarmed into two who'd been brawling all their desperate lives.

A haymaker crunched against the side of Mitchell's head, seeming to come from nowhere. Knocked momentarily clear of the fierce scrum, he had a blurred glimpse of two figures standing some thirty feet away in the yard before Joachim howled a warning and he ducked not a split second too soon as Clyde barely missed with a sweeping blow of his sixgun.

He straightened and hammered the man backwards with a vicious straight right.

'Step aside, boys!' a harsh voice roared from the corner. 'The Judas is mine!'

It was Jackson. The ugly Diamond-backer had come running from inside to slide into a low crouch in the mud. The Ponyleg in his fist stabbed a red finger of death at a diving Big Max before a panting Mitchell could bring his cutter up, with Clyde and Frick diving low. The shot went wild. The bullet tore off the heel of Frick's boot. Jackson cursed and was depressing the trigger of his Ponyleg for the second time when Mitchell and Joachim fired in unison.

The badman fell on his back and didn't even kick.

As though enraged by the necessity of what they'd had to do, the trio were upon Frick and Clyde before they could regain their footing. The wide and vicious sweep of the sixgun in Big Max's hand terminated with a sicken-ing crunching sound at the back of Clyde's skull and the man somersaulted twice from the terrible impact before hitting the wall.

Frick almost got his gun working but

almost wasn't enough. Bootheels sucked in yellow mud as three angry men hammered a fourth, firstly to his knees, then unconscious on to the broad of his back where a white-faced Big Max couldn't resist driving in one last kick.

★　★　★

Spitting blood, breath tearing in his lungs, Cord swung lurchingly to face the north wing, squinting through tatters of gunsmoke for a long agonizing moment until the wind gusted and he saw the couple clearly. Udo and Connie locked together facing him from twenty feet away, and she was alive.

His heart skipped with relief.

Connie was still alive and seemingly unharmed as she continued to struggle weakly in Udo's grasp. Then he stiffened as the gunman's mad eye picked him out through the smoke, and he thrust his gun muzzle harder up beneath Connie's straining jaw.

'Let her go, Udo!' a bloody-faced Stein bawled over Cord's shoulder. 'The boys are finished and there's only you left now. Let the lady go and you can hightail, that's the best I can offer.'

'Go straight to hell!' Udo snarled. His stare was demonic. 'You're in no shape to offer one damn thing, you turncoat son of a bitch. You know, I knew from the jump that you were a two-faced rat, Stein . . . knew that no psalm-singing sonuva who ever switches to the other side, even for a day, much less five years, can ever be trusted again. Well, you lose again, Maxy.' He gestured with the gun. 'C'mon, losers, get the boys on their feet and get out the buckboard on account of I hold all the cards and you don't have no option. Am I telling it how it is or not, Mitchell, you mongrel?'

He started giggling, but broke off as big Frick clawed his bloody way up on to one knee and blinked in his direction.

'They . . . they ain't going to let us

just go, Telly . . . ' His voice was a croak. He was one sick hardcase. He gestured and almost toppled. 'Look . . . lawdogs up there, Max and these hardnoses here . . . folks'll be showing up from the town soon to see what all the shooting's about.' With a huge effort the man struggled to his feet. He looked like the victim of a train wreck, but he was making sense. 'The game's over. Let's take a piece of what they're offering, man.'

For a teetering moment that seemed more like an eternity, they watched fugitive emotions chase one another across Telly Udo's wild-eyed face. But no man dared move, for such was the frightening intensity in the man's eyes that it seemed Udo might butcher his hostage before their very eyes. He might well have done but for the sudden eruption of violence above and behind, causing him to jerk his head towards the windows of the north wing room where all hell was breaking loose.

A desperate Lino had eventually

broken free to dive upon Hanline, using his heavy chair as a club to smash the man unconscious. Lino's hope was to snatch the all-important key and bust out through the rear window into the darkness before Prade could react. He got as far as closing his fingers over the key-ring before a gunbutt slammed the back of his head once, again. As the outlaw slumped across the unconscious deputy, Prade lunged back to his window in time to see Udo, beginning to shiver to his own insane laughter again, now dragging his hostage away towards the wing.

Udo saw him momentarily exposed. His gun bucked once and the marshal fell with a crash as Mitchell's hoarse shout carried across the yard.

'Hold up, Udo. Where the hell do you think you're going?'

'Leaving is what, you son of a whore!' Udo was nothing if not flexible. The abject failure of his henchmen and the brutal reality of both Max and the handyman backing Mitchell's play, told him with knife-edged clarity that the main game was lost. But not over. He would survive.

He always did.

'I'm high-tailing and she's going with me, drifter.'

'No!' Cord lunged from cover involuntarily and Udo fired in the same instant. The bullet slammed Cord's shoulder, driving him back where Big Max and Joachim were able to seize him and drag him to safety. When Stein peered around the corner again, of killer and hostage there was no sign.

'Try to follow and she is meat, you scumsuckin' bastards!'

The fading sound of Udo's taunt batted between hotel and barn as Cord lurched erect, head cocked and a cold sweat gleaming along the cut of his jaw.

'He's heading for the jetty,' he groaned. 'The boat . . . ?'

All three were hurt yet still managed to traverse the eighty-foot length of the hotel's façade in time to see dim figures vanish round the first brushy bend in the pathway leading to the jetty.

'He'll kill her if we go after him,' panted Big Max.

'And kill her if we don't,' Mitchell groaned. Then they were running, together, staggering and bleeding, each carrying his own burden of fear and guilt which united them in a strange, strong way, big Max Stein no less than his companions.

They were approaching the corner when a scream of total agony ripped through the dark skies causing them to pause momentarily before rushing on at breakneck speed. Beyond the corner lay fifty yards of empty sodden pathway leading to the small boatshed that marked the end of the obscured jetty.

Mitchell was first to come skidding round the boatshed on to the slick jetty-boards, where he lunged to a horrified halt. A short distance ahead, a slim figure stretched on the planking with another against the railing a short distance beyond. No. Another two. Dashing at his eyes, he focused on the supine, motionless shape stretched out face up to the rain, horrified and certain it had to be Connie. But his joints seemed frozen, refusing to carry him forward.

Then a faint cry. 'Cord. Is that you, Cord?'

Her voice!

As his companions rushed up behind he went lunging forward, focusing on the two figures beyond that supine and bloodied shape — one slender, one bulky.

'Crow Woman!' Joachim croaked hoarsely at his back. 'Miz Connie with her . . . I think . . . '

'Then what . . . ?' Cord switched his attention to that frozen shape. His voice gave out. Now he was close enough to see that it was Udo, stone dead and glassy-eyed with the ghastly lips of his gaping, slashed throat smiling up at the sky and the haft of a big heavy knife protruding from his ripped belly.

Joachim was half-laughing with pride, half-sobbing with pain as he said, 'Told you there was nobody better with a knife than my gal, didn't I?'

But Mitchell didn't hear. Connie was suddenly in his arms, sobbing out all the words he knew he'd wanted to hear all his life. All the things he had felt himself, but had never been able to say. Never had a woman he could say them to until this moment.

Then at a warning cry from Big Max, all three whirled and a nimble Crow Woman darted to retrieve her fierce blade from the killer's corpse. Swift pounding steps drew closer beyond the boatshed and moments later the bow-legged figure came rushing into sight, head tilted back, arms pumping, running with a real high knee action.

The runner skidded, stumbled and almost fell when he saw everybody — and the big guns. Even brother-in-law Big Max had Lino up in his sights as they blocked his way to the *Rafaela*, and his brother and sister — his last desperate hope for freedom and life.

It was all too much for Lino

Caballero Guardia, who yet again in his colorful career had just bucked all the odds to display his skill and ratlike cunning and fighting heart to prevail against his enemies, so hungry was he for his freedom and for life.

It seemed perfectly in character that the pride of Mexico and the scourge of Texas should fall to his bony knees and begin to weep.

★　★　★

The moon was bright and the high seas off the Laguna Madre were theirs alone as the good ship *Rafaela* nosed her way southwards through the gentle swell.

Miguel emerged from the wheelhouse, wiping his hands on his chinos, cap at a jaunty angle and big teeth flashing. He clapped his hands in time to the music as brother Lino and sister Evalina, so heavy with child yet so light on her feet, danced and swayed on the moving deck to the strains of Big Max's harmonica.

He threw his skinny arms at the sky and cried, 'It is a miracle, and may the Virgin be praised and may the tongue of Miguel rot out if he ever says one cruel word against any gringo ever again. Viva Señor Mitchell and Señor Joachim and Señora Crow Woman, saint of the sacred blade. *Olé!*'

The dancers joined in the wild cheering and Big Max smiled like a benevolent patriarch surrounded by his happy children, marvelling at how sweet life could be, and how surprising.

Of course it had looked bad for a while back there on the jetty. Real bad, and threatening to turn disastrous. For all were guilty; Lino of getting caught by his Texan enemies initially; Big Max himself for setting out to stage his impossible rescue operation in the name of the family; Miguel for taking part in the risky operation and Evalina for lending her inspiring presence and according her blessing to the whole crazy venture.

Men had died, there would be chaos

and confusion at the hotel right now with serious repercussions to inevitably follow the mayhem. And yet they dared still hope all would be well, even believed it would prove so.

Such was their faith in Señor Mitchell and Señora Wheeler now.

It was Mitchell who'd observed the wildly emotional reunion between the Guardias and their rogue brother, and slowly came to realize to just what heroic and selfless extremes expatriate Big Max had been prepared to go to on behalf of 'my brother and the uncle of my unborn child' as he'd put it.

And had begun to waver.

The more he saw, heard and thought the clearer seemed his thinking, and he soon heard himself thinking out loud with Connie squeezing his hands and nodding encouragement, thus giving the party from Mexico their first glimmer of hope.

The way Cord Mitchell evaluated the situation as of that moment — seeking and finding a way through a maze of emotion and threatening danger — seemed simplicity itself.

And what stood out in stark simplicity was that should all be turned over to the authorities it would mean prison, misery and endless court cases for all concerned up to and even probably including himself. Whereas if they were to simply disappear, and he was able to clear the area of incriminating evidence, such as badmen and corpses, before Marshal Prade and his junior could recover and intervene, then Thief Creek Hotel might be left with what would be a lot of fuss, uproar and suspicion on the part of the authorities, yet with maybe a better than even chance of surviving it and returning to the normal everyday life they craved and felt they richly deserved.

'There's no fault here,' he pronounced with mounting assurance. 'The *Regulares* shouldn't have jailed Lino, Max shouldn't have broken the law to save him, Udo shouldn't have happened to anybody. But it's over and

226

done and I'm damned if I intend seeing good people punished over things they weren't initially responsible for. There's been enough punishment and bloodshed tonight to satisfy Storm Bay for the century . . . so why are you people just standing here in the rain?'

Excitement beyond belief was the response he got when they realized just what he was proposing, and there was barely time for the handshakes and kisses and the last farewells. They put swiftly to sea . . . just in case their 'gringo saviours' should perhaps change their minds.

Too late now if they did.

Standing bow-legged and sturdy on the deck facing the distant Texas coastline, Lino Guardia scratched behind his ears and tugged at his generous nose. Every sea-mile they journeyed carried them that much further from the gallows. Soon he would be back safely in San Bonito once again, where even the *Federales* treated him as a great man. He would parade the plazas and the *señoritas* would throw themselves at his feet while all Mexico and Los Estados Unitos marvelled at the great Lino's latest great escape.

Of course he would surely go down on his knees every day of his life to thank Jesus for his delivery from his enemies, but there was one small concern nagging at the back of his mind where his vanity lived. For what would they say, and how might they laugh — even in Catarina — should they know exactly how it was he had been set free?

Only his brother really knew Lino for both his great strength and many weaknesses, and paramount amongst the latter was his almost childish vanity. And should it ever become known that in the end the great Caballero had only survived due to the generosity and courage of a bunch of Texans — his mortal enemies — then surely the scornful laughter would never end.

'Have no fears, my brother,' Miguel

grinned hugely, knowingly. 'For upon our return, Miguel shall tell all Benito that you alone saved Señora Wheeler and that you gunned down all the evil *bandidos* single-handed whilst the rest of us lay ill with the fever below decks.' He chuckled and squeezed hard. 'Now you are happy, *compañero*?'

The huge smile on the face of the Hero of Catarina said it all.

★ ★ ★

Their new married quarters were finished now. A covered breezeway separated the construction from the hotel. A new horse barn had also been erected and, over by Thief Creek, the spring house and corrals were coming along. Summer was near. The morning was crisp. A dew lay shining on the grass.

Mitchell turned away from his wife at the sound of wheels to see yet another coachload of curious sightseers rolling in for one of Joachim's increasingly famous Texas brunches. The notoriety of that violent night had placed the Thief Creek Hotel on the map, and visitors liked to poke their fingers in the bullet holes and listen to Joachim give his version of what had happened, which in no way resembled the official report on the incident to which a somewhat dazed and confused Marshal Prade had finally signed his name.

The lawmen didn't stop by any longer. There seemed no point. From Mitchell down to little Jody, their recollection of events covering the gun battle and the subsequent flight of the outlaws with their dead and wounded, although sketchy and vague, seemed watertight.

In reality, Owl Marsh had swallowed the dead, while the hardcase survivors had been let run. Not legal. But it had worked and was still working for Mitchell and his people.

He smiled.

Now with Big Max and his gang vanished as though the earth had swallowed them, and Lino Guardia very publicly back in Mexico, Cord heard vague rumours that Prade planned to quit, and go to Mexico after El Caballero as a private citizen, but doubted he ever would.

He wanted life to be good for Big Max, the man to whom he owed a great debt. For Stein had done long ago what he himself was doing now. Had cut himself off from the old wild ways to be with the woman he loved, then shown it could work. He'd advised Mitchell how he should go about matters that night on the jetty before they set sail, the wisest words this drifter had ever heard.

Gracias, Max. And thank you, Connie.

All his life until now he'd never understood what kept him gambling and drinking his way from one town to another, yet understood with crystal clarity now why he'd always be here in this place, with this woman.

We do hope that you have enjoyed reading this large print book.

Did you know that all of our titles are available for purchase?

We publish a wide range of high quality large print books including:
Romances, Mysteries, Classics
General Fiction
Non Fiction and Westerns

Special interest titles available in large print are:
The Little Oxford Dictionary
Music Book, Song Book
Hymn Book, Service Book

Also available from us courtesy of Oxford University Press:
Young Readers' Dictionary
(large print edition)
Young Readers' Thesaurus
(large print edition)

For further information or a free brochure, please contact us at:
Ulverscroft Large Print Books Ltd.,
The Green, Bradgate Road, Anstey,
Leicester, LE7 7FU, England.
Tel: (00 44) **0116 236 4325**
Fax: (00 44) **0116 234 0205**

Other titles in the
Linford Western Library:

MIDNIGHT LYNCHING

Terry Murphy

When Ruby Malone's husband is lynched by a sheriff's posse, Wells Fargo investigator Asa Harker goes after the beautiful widow expecting her to lead him to the vast sum of money stolen from his company. But Ruby has gone on the outlaw trail with the handsome, young Ben Whitman. Worse still, Harker finds he must deal with a crooked sheriff. Without help, it looks as if he will not only fail to recover the stolen money but also lose his life into the bargain.

BRAZOS STATION

Clayton Nash

Caleb Brett liked his job as deputy sheriff and being betrothed to the sheriff's daughter, Rose. What he didn't like was the thought of the sheriff moving in with them once they were married. But capturing the infamous outlaw Gil Bannerman offered a way out because there was plenty of reward money. Then came Brett's big mistake — he lost Bannerman and was framed. Now everything he treasured was lost. Did he have a chance in hell of fighting his way back?